Wicked Force

Wicked Force
By Sawyer Bennett

A Wicked Horse Vegas/Big Sky Novella

Introduction by Kristen Proby

EVIL EYE
CONCEPTS

Wicked Force: A Wicked Horse Vegas/Big Sky Novella
By Sawyer Bennett
Copyright 2019
ISBN: 978-1-970077-07-0

Published by Evil Eye Concepts, Incorporated

This is a work of fiction. Names, places, characters and incidents are the product of the author's imagination and are fictitious. Any resemblance to actual persons, living or dead, events or establishments is solely coincidental.

An Introduction to the Kristen Proby Crossover Collection

Everyone knows there's nothing I love more than a happy ending. It's what I do for a living–I'm in LOVE with love. And what's better than love? More love, of course!

Just imagine, Louis Vuitton and Tiffany, collaborating on the world's most perfect handbag. Jimmy Choo and Louboutin, making shoes just for me. Not loving it enough? What if Hugh Grant in *Notting Hill* was the man to barge into Sandra Bullock's office in *The Proposal*? I think we can all agree that Julia Roberts' character would have had her hands full with Ryan Reynolds.

Now imagine what would happen if one of the characters from my Big Sky Series met up with other characters from some of your favorite authors' series. Well, wonder no more because The Kristen Proby Crossover Collection is here, and I could not be more excited!

Rachel Van Dyken, Laura Kaye, Sawyer Bennett, Monica Murphy, Samantha Young, and K.L. Grayson are all bringing their own beloved characters to play – and find their happy endings – in my world. Can you imagine all the love, laughter and shenanigans in store?

I hope you enjoy the journey between worlds!

Love,
Kristen Proby

The Kristen Proby Crossover Collection features a new novel by Kristen Proby and six by some of her favorite writers:

Kristen Proby – Soaring with Fallon
Sawyer Bennett – Wicked Force
KL Grayson – Crazy Imperfect Love
Laura Kaye – Worth Fighting For
Monica Murphy – Nothing Without You
Rachel Van Dyken – All Stars Fall
Samantha Young – Hold On

Chapter 1

Kynan

Jerico must really want something big from me to spring for such an extravagant meal. It's not the first time I've eaten at The Ledbury but I definitely don't make it a habit. Trendy Notting Hill fine dining isn't high up on my list of things that make my world go round.

But Jerico knows that. He and I have shared many an MRE in the hills of Afghanistan as our country's military forces combined and worked together to flush the Taliban out. We're both former marines but Jerico served the stars and stripes and I served the Queen of England. Just as our countries were strong allies, so too were Jerico and I.

I approach the maître d's podium and smile at the lovely blonde behind it. "8PM reservation. Jameson."

"Of course, Mr. McGrath," she replies with an elegant incline of her head that doesn't match the East End, Cockney accent that she tries to hide. "Mr. Jameson is already seated. If you'll follow me."

It's no chore following the blonde who is wearing a simple black but well-fit dress through the restaurant. I keep my eyes pinned on her arse as we weave our way through tables set with the finest china and crystal available in London.

I almost run into the back of the woman when she comes to a stop beside a table that could hold four but is set for two. My gaze regretfully leaves her backside and I focus in on my buddy, Jerico Jameson, sitting there. He smirks at me, no doubt probably having watched me ogle the woman as we walked his way.

"Here you are," the hostess says, and I give her a nod of thanks.

Jerico stands up as she pivots to leave and holds his hand out to me. I grip it hard, not to crush it but to pull him to me for a quick half-hug where we mutually pound each other on the back. We last saw each other over a year ago at Camp Leatherneck in the Helmand Province. I was shipping back to the Royal Marine base at Bickleigh Barracks, home to 42 Commando, where I'd served for the last six years.

When I'd left, Jerico was heading back out with his unit for more reconnaissance operations to locate insurgents. We'd, of course, stayed in contact and I was more than thrilled when he called to say he was in London and wanted to get together.

I release Jerico and he grins at me. "Did I detect you getting a little soft under that suit coat?"

Snorting, I unbutton said suit coat and pull a chair out to take a seat. "Let's hit the gym tomorrow and compare bench presses, mate."

Jerico laughs and sits down opposite me. "You actually look real good, Kynan. Civilian life agrees with you."

I snort again because it most certainly doesn't agree with me. While I knew I didn't want to stay in the military anymore, I also have come to realize that I don't want to continue working for my father's luxury car dealership. While joining the family business is a fine way to spend my time until I figure out what the fuck I want to do in life, I'm not going to make a career out of wiping dust off Aston Martins sprawled across the showroom floor.

"I take it you're not enjoying life as a car salesman," Jerico ventures and then raises his hand to get a waiter's attention.

"Yeah, not my life's ambition," I admit but say no more as the server approaches.

Jerico orders a scotch and I order a beer. When we're alone again, I ask him, "And what have you been up to since you got out?"

Mostly we stay in contact via email with a few calls in between. I know Jerico officially got out of the marine corps just a few months ago, but I wasn't sure what he'd been doing since.

"It's funny you should ask," he says as he leans casually back in his chair, placing one forearm on the table. "Because I'm here to offer you a job."

My eyebrows snap upward. "What kind of job?"

Jerico shoots me a sly smile. "I thought we'd shoot the shit a bit and catch up on each other's lives but if you want me to jump right in...?"

I'm not one to waste time. "Let's not wag off. Tell me what you got."

Expression turning serious, Jerico leans forward to put both arms on the table. "I'm starting up a security services firm. I have some financial backing and you're the first person I'm offering a job to."

I study him for a moment, noting the way his dark green eyes are unflinching as they stay pinned on me. "Security services can mean a lot of things. Give me a little more detail."

Jerico shrugs. "Could be something as simple as protection services or security consultations."

"And something as complex as...?"

He shrugs again but I don't miss the twinkle in his eye. "Contract work for the government."

"Whose government?" I press.

"Yours, mine, someone else's," he says nonchalantly.

I can read between the lines. He's talking covert operations for hire by agencies like the CIA or MI6. That could be rescues or assassinations or any number of things in between. While I don't need him to spell out those details to me, I do need to be assured we're on the right side of things.

"What are your hard limits?" I ask him.

Jerico looks genuinely hurt I'd ask such a thing. "I won't take candy from kids if that's what you mean."

I just stare at him.

There's a flash of white teeth as he laughs at me. "Only white hat stuff. Saving people, helping to fight terrorism."

That I could work with.

"We only assassinate really bad guys," he adds.

That gives me pause and he must see it on my face because he raises both hands up in mock surrender to indicate he's done teasing me. "The only government contracts I'm interested in are ones in which we'd be joining up with special ops forces. Things that are sanctioned by our governments and where they might need extra support. Those bring in high dollar compared to the risk. But honestly, I want to build the company up with a lot of domestic type of work. Like I said, security services, armed protection. Stuff like that."

"And I'm the first you contacted?" I ask him, and I'm not sure why that's so important to me. I know Jerico has worked with a lot of high-level military during his short career as a marine and probably has a lot of mates he's closer to than me.

Yet here he is in London buying me a fancy dinner.

"Your experience in human intelligence is a plus, but you're the first I asked because you're the one I'd trust the most with my life," he tells me, and then pulls an envelope out of the inside breast pocket of his suit coat.

Leaning forward, he hands it across the table to me at the same time our waiter returns with our drinks. Jerico picks up his scotch but I ignore my beer as I break the seal and pull out a document titled "Offer of Employment."

I take my time to read it, noting that the salary and benefits far exceed what I could make working at a luxury car dealership. But the risk is greater too, so most of the money is considered hazardous duty pay.

"That offer to you is confidential as I'm not offering those same exact terms to other recruits," Jerico says blandly. "But—"

"But I'll also be the first you'll call up for something dangerous." I finish his sentence as I fold the document back up and slide it into the envelope. Setting it down on the table, I pick up my beer and take a sip. "It's a good offer. Great even."

"Yes, it is," Jerico agrees.

"Where are you going to have your main offices?"

"Vegas," he says and I blink in surprise, because I figured he'd locate closer to Washington, D.C., if we were going to be doing contract work for the government.

Jerico chuckles. "Seriously, Kynan... most of the work is going to stay domestic. It's not going to be uber exciting stuff. Trust me, after you have to guard some pop diva princess for a few days, you're going to be begging me to send you on a dark op. The truth is though, it's a higher return on investment to build up a volume of private security work with less risk to us."

"Then why do contract work at all?" I ask him.

Jerico shrugs and gives me a sly grin. "Because that money is very, very good and I'll personally need something to combat the boredom of protecting pop diva princesses."

I turn back to the issue of being headquartered in Vegas as it's not my favorite place in the world. "Why Las Vegas?"

"Because my first private contract I have in place is to upgrade the security on three major casinos owned by a large consortium," he tells me. "It's enough money to completely fund startup expenses and salaries for a full five years. The project will take months and the tax breaks are really good."

"Damn." I blow out a low whistle of appreciation. "How did you score that? You're not even in business yet."

"Let's just say the CEO of the consortium owes me a huge favor."

I cock an eyebrow at Jerico. He can't leave me hanging like that.

He grins. "I served with his son and had an occasion to save his life. His dad is eternally grateful. But I had to put in a legit bid on the project and compete with some other security firms. Still, it was the boon owed to me that pushed the odds in my favor."

I take a moment to consider what I've learned. A damn good offer of employment that lets me do what I'm good at. While I didn't want to serve in the Royal Marines for the span of a life career, I did love the work. And while private security might be as dull as selling luxury cars, I can read enough between the lines with Jerico. We're going to have some jobs that are going to pay insanely well and will satisfy our need for adrenaline rushes. I'm an admitted adrenaline junkie and this sounds right up my alley.

"I hate Vegas," I tell Jerico and he snorts. I can't help but laugh. "But I like your offer and I'll gladly accept. When do you want me to start?"

Jerico's face lights up with relief and I truly understand just how much he must respect my abilities. "As soon as you can, buddy. We have some casinos to fortify."

I pick up my beer and hold it out. He does the same with his scotch and we tap the glasses against each other.

"Cheers, mate," I tell him with a smile. "Here's to a great new adventure for us."

"Cheers," he replies and tips his glass back.

Chapter 2

Joslyn

The last lingering notes fade away and the applause is instantaneously thunderous. My arms are stretched high in the air for a victorious moment, one clutching the wireless microphone and the other waving to the crowd. The relief that I pulled off another successful show pulses through my body.

It's funny how that fear never goes away.

Every time I step onto a stage, I'm terrified of being a complete failure. I have nightmares where my voice sounds like a frog croaking or I get paralyzed by the bright lights as people just stare at me. I have no clue if all people in show business feel that way, but it's the total downside to my career.

I bring my free hand to my mouth, touch my lips to my fingertips, and blow the kiss out to the crowd. The cheers get louder and I take a low bow.

Another kiss to the crowd.

Another bow as I bask in their appreciation just a little bit longer.

Then I exit stage right, waving to the crowd and beaming my smile at them as I depart.

When I'm finally out of sight, the smile slides off my face and my legs turn to jelly. The adrenaline rush having been expended, I'm as limp as a noodle.

Michel is there to put an arm around my waist, not to hold me up, but to give me a squeeze of excitement. "Joslyn... another fantastic show."

Yes, it was and that brings a smile back to my face because despite all the fears and insecurities, I freaking love singing to people. I wrap my arm around his waist and we walk together back to my dressing room.

Michel is my hair and makeup guru and has been for the past nine months since I signed a one-year contract to perform here in Vegas. He's also my closest friend, and that's not something I've had a lot of over the past few years.

His real name is Michael Brubank and he's from New Jersey. At the tender age of twenty, he completed cosmetology school and moved out to L.A., where he changed his name to Michel.

Not Michel Brubank.

Just Michel.

Like Madonna or Cher.

After several years in L.A. working his way up the ladder of famous and semi-famous stars, he came to Vegas because he was in love with an interior designer he'd met online and dated long distance.

Sadly, he and the interior designer didn't work out but Michel fell in love with Vegas and stayed. I'm only nineteen and Michel is now thirty-one, yet the vast age difference between us hasn't interfered with our friendship. We're both in show business, he loves to gossip and I love to listen, and he's got a heart the size of Texas. He'd do anything for me and I for him, and thus we're the best of friends.

"Be warned," he leans over and murmurs as we approach my dressing room. "She's not in a good mood."

"What did I do now?" I mutter as my body tightens with defensiveness.

"Who knows," he whispers back, afraid to let his voice carry any further than our little cocoon as we stop outside the door. The name Joslyn Meyers in gold letters with a gold star underneath usually makes me smile, but not right now.

Taking a deep breath—pushing past the tightness now in my chest—I release my arm from around Michel's waist and give him a confident smile. "I'll call you later after I get home, okay?"

There's no hiding the worry in his eyes. "You sure you don't want me to go in there with you? I'll get your makeup off and brush your hair out."

I go to my tiptoes because Michel is quite tall and give him a kiss to his cheek. "I'm fine. I'll call you later."

"Okay," he says doubtfully and chucks me under the chin with his knuckles. "And no matter what happens in there, just remember you are fabulous."

"You're the fabulous one," I say and he preens from the compliment.

Laughing, I watch as Michel heads off and then take another deep breath as I turn toward the door to my dressing room. Exhaling slowly, I open it and step across the threshold with my head held confidently high.

"You put me in a really bad position, Joslyn," my stepmother says as she taps a manicured nail against her chin.

I take her in.

All of the glory of Madeline Meyers as she leans back against my dressing room table.

Maddie to her dear friends, which number zero, because like me, she doesn't really have any. Also like me, her life has been overtaken by show business as she manages my career. She's statuesque, with glossy brunette hair she wears in a long bob, a flawless complexion, and an incomparable sense of style. She wears the title of Manager to Joslyn Meyers like it's a superhero cape and she takes her job almost too seriously.

Before I devote another thought to my stepmother, please let me make it clear. She's not evil or wicked. On the contrary, she's been so very good to me for much of my life and I love her.

But she is... trying.

Frustrating.

Overbearing.

Good intentioned but often tormenting because she's a bulldog in her tenacity to make me famous.

I consider playing stupid with her, but that will only piss her off to the point we'll get into a terrible argument and then I'll feel wretched over it. So I go ahead and admit my perfidy.

"I'm sorry," I tell her with true feeling. I am regretful to have done something she was firmly opposed to, because I know it causes her stress. But I have no qualms about what I did, because it was the right thing to do and because it brings *me* joy. "This was really important to me, Mom."

Yes, I call her "Mom" because she's always been that to me, except when we are in front of others for business dealings. She thinks it weakens her position to shine light onto our personal relationship.

Her lips purse and she regards me through unhappy eyes. "You ruined a very nice deal I was putting together for you. It was going to be a stepping stone to the next level in your career. You've taken a lot of hard work that I had put into it and totally disrespected my efforts by accepting the Cunningham Falls event."

"I know," I say softly. All true accusations against me but I've already made my apology.

"Joslyn," she snaps at me and my spine stiffens. "That's all you have to say? Do you understand how hard I work for you? The promises I have to make and the back scratching that goes on to get you ahead in this world?"

I remain silent because there's no argument to be made.

Her voice goes almost shrill. "I have only your best interests at heart and everything I do is for your happiness and success. And I can't continue doing that if you undermine me. You've made me look weak now to people in the industry and you've made it a hundred times harder for me to negotiate anything on your behalf. Because now everyone will think I have a willful, bratty diva daughter who can't be controlled. No one will want to work with you."

Biting hard on the inside of my cheek, I let the anger wash through me but I refuse to engage with her. My mom has a sharp tongue and an even greater ability to throw massive guilt on my shoulders that makes me feel so weighted I can't breathe.

The source of this disagreement is my acceptance to headline a charity concert back in my hometown of Cunningham Falls, Montana. My mom did not want me to do this because—as noted—she was putting together a much better deal for me that conflicted.

One that involved a paycheck. I'm sure part of her discontent is that I'm doing the concert for free, but mostly I knew that by accepting this event I was going to be ruining other plans she was deep into the process of making for the benefit of my career.

Putting her palms to the edge of my dressing table, she pushes off and pivots away from me. I watch silently as she walks to the small refrigerator and pulls out a bottle of coconut water. I grimace as she twists the top off and hands it over to me. I step forward and reluctantly take it.

She nods toward it, her voice soft and solicitous. "Drink up. You know it's good for you."

Funny how everything she thinks is good for me and pushes on me—be it coconut water, beet smoothies or kale salads—is all stuff that I can't stand.

When I raise the bottle to my lips, allowing just a tiny bit of the foul liquid in my mouth, she gives me a soft smile as she inclines her head. "You know I only want what's best for you, right?"

I nod, and I truly believe that.

"And do you trust that the decisions I'm making for your career are for your sole benefit?"

Another nod, because again... I believe her intentions are pure. She's done an amazing job so far in managing my career and has worked relentlessly to get me where I am.

My mom's voice gentles even more. "Then please trust me when I say the Cunningham Falls concert is a bad idea and you need to send your regrets. Tell them you have a schedule conflict you didn't realize when you accepted or something like that."

I shake my head, my expression both apologetic but resolved. "I can't. I made a promise but more than that, I want to do this. This is personally important to me."

Her visage turns wounded, the corners of her mouth pulling down. Tears form in her eyes. "You don't think that charity is important to me too? After everything I went through with your father? After everything I did, you don't think I would really love you to do that concert for charity?"

And there it is.

The guilt trip. It strikes me true and deep, causing my stomach to cramp and my heart to constrict.

My birth mother died in childbirth so I never knew her. Only stories from my dad and a brief history of photos he had from their all too short relationship. He married Madeline when I was six years old and she joined forces with him to raise me. I was so hungry for a mother figure, I called her "Mom" from the moment they got married.

My dad adored her and she him. She adored me and I her. We were a good family together, even if her tendencies to be overbearing were always something my dad and I had to accept. She was the boss in the family and we did what she told us to do. My dad was a pushover and I followed his example.

Regardless, she was a good mom as I grew up and she's the one who encouraged me to pursue my passion for singing. She took me to lessons and competitions and sewed me fancy costumes. She researched the best foods and supplements to make sure I stayed healthy and monitored my diet and exercise with the vigilance of a drill instructor. Madeline Meyers is very much the reason I'm standing where I am today.

But more than anything—the real reason I will be truly grateful to her and will usually always, always bend to her will—is that she cared for my dad while he died from cancer. She drove him to all his treatments, monitored his medications, did endless research for alternative therapies, and when things got really bad at the end, she was the one who did everything. She was the one who never left the side of the hospital bed set up in our living room by hospice. She emptied his catheter bag and cleaned him when he soiled himself. She gave him baths and changed his sheets and rubbed ice over his lips. When he slipped into unconsciousness, she kept up an endless stream of dialogue so he knew that she was still there.

I was there too. I did some of those things and helped her with much of it. But I also had breaks. I went out with friends to get away. I was able to have some respite, but not my mom. She was there 100% with him to the very end and I owe her everything for it.

Except for this. I'm doing this charity concert—benefiting cancer research—and I'm doing it because my father loved Cunningham Falls passionately. While it was too small to suit me or my stepmom for long term purposes, it was a part of who my father was, as his family had lived there for generations.

"Mom," I say quietly. "You will never know how much I appreciate everything you do. I couldn't be what I am without you. But I am doing this concert. It's important to me and I'm not going to budge on it. I'm so sorry for the extra work this will cause you, but I also know you will figure a way to salvage whatever you were working on or in the alternative, find something even better."

Her lips flatten as her shoulders slump in defeat, knowing that even the memory of what a saint she was with my father isn't going to sway me this time. She knows that I've had a very rare win in a battle against her.

"Fine," she finally says with a long sigh. "I'll see what I can do."

"Thank you," I whisper but the smile she gives in return is dull.

Eyes filled with disappointment, she nods at my water. "Now drink up and let's get you home. Don't forget we have an early meeting tomorrow with that security company I want to hire."

I'm so relieved she's given up fighting me on the concert that I put the coconut water to my mouth and start to suck every nasty drop of it down.

Chapter 3

Kynan

I pace the lobby of our office building waiting for my 10AM appointment to arrive. I was forced to put on a suit today which I hate, but Jerico asked me to meet with a new prospective client because he was otherwise tied up in meetings in Washington, D.C. I'm waiting in the lobby because we have not hired a receptionist yet. Our client base is too small at this time to justify the expense, but that's about to change.

Jerico told me he had financial backing to start this business in addition to the huge casino contract we've been working on for the last three months since he convinced me to move to Vegas to work for him. He's been in D.C. a lot so I have to assume some of the financial backing is coming from that part of the country. My guess is he's been hired to assist in some type of covert operation—with most likely the CIA—and thus I'm here meeting clients.

Our offices are definitely unique. The interior is all dark paneled walls, cream marble flooring, and high-end furniture. The outside looks like a fortress.

He bought a three-story building in downtown Las Vegas that was in foreclosure. The outside is composed of white concrete and to the casual observer driving by, it looks like there are no windows. Just solid concrete from top to bottom.

On closer inspection, though, there are rectangular windows that go floor to ceiling on each level that are frosted on the outside to match the exterior.

It looks strong and intimidating on the approach, but step inside and it's elegant and warm. I'm guessing Jerico wants his civilian clients to feel comfortable and since most of them are extremely wealthy, he paid a great deal of money to an expensive interior designer to make it so.

My favorite part, though, is a small, discreet silver sign on the main lobby door that reads "The Jameson Group - International Security Services." It reminds me that in addition to babysitting pop princesses, I will be doing some adrenaline-inducing jobs as well.

I glance at my watch, noting that our very first client could be walking in the door at any minute. For the past three months, we've been working non-stop on the casino properties. After hiring me and another marine buddy of his, Jayce Barnes, he went on to recruit another twelve security professionals to join his business. But that project is going to be winding down and he wants to start building up a name in domestic protection services.

Yay. I get to be a bodyguard.

Glancing at my watch again, I wonder if Joslyn Meyers is punctual or doesn't care about wasting people's time. My preconception about any star—be it actor, singer, or politician—is that they mostly don't care about keeping others waiting.

I did my research before today's meeting because I wanted to know what I'd be facing. Jerico wants to land this contract and even though he has a strong personal recommendation behind him, it's going to be up to me to seal the deal.

Joslyn Meyers is an interesting story, no doubt. Nineteen years old and probably on a trajectory to stardom. She won a national talent competition—one of those ones that are on TV with celebrity hosts that help them to compete against others week to week—and scored a recording contract. She put out an album but sadly, it had lackluster sales and she wasn't offered a second one.

She wasn't defeated though. Joslyn was offered a Vegas contract to perform at one of the major theaters here, where she puts on a show that appeals to a broad base audience. She sings some of her own songs and does amazing covers of legendary artists, and somehow manages to combine in unparalleled choreography with a slew of backup dancers. I understand it's quite an entertainment spectacle.

So that's her story. My guess is she'll move on from Vegas at some point, but here she is now. And apparently needing security services, although I can't understand why. It's not like she's a huge mega star or anything.

When the front door opens, spilling in a little morning light across the creamy marble foyer, I brace myself. That's because in my research of Joslyn Meyers, the most disgruntling thing I learned about her was that she was a stunningly gorgeous creature with immense talent. If you weren't swayed to fall in love with her voice, you only had to take one look at her face and body to succumb.

She's got platinum blonde hair, so light it's almost silvery. It falls in long, wavy lengths to the middle of her back and swoops down across her forehead, highlighting the angelic lines of her face. It's absolutely perfect. Not a single thing out of place that would make her seem a bit more real and less like a fairytale princess. Joslyn has the bluest of eyes, pale and shimmering. Her lips are full and inspire a million dirty thoughts. Her body is slamming and I know this because in the research I did, I watched videos of her Vegas act and there's little left to the imagination when it comes to her costumes.

In totality, she's the perfect woman and I'm a sucker for such things. The only thing I can hope for is that her personality sucks so I won't be attracted to her. Despite what many women think, it's not all about looks.

Not that I'm overly worried about it. I mean, she is just a job.

A job that I am absolutely prohibited from banging, no matter how much I might want to because she's fucking hot as hell.

I shake my head and force my thoughts out of the gutter and back into business mode. But then she steps into the lobby and my body goes tight upon seeing her. She's half turned away from me, talking to someone walking in behind her. No clue who it is because I can't take my eyes off Joslyn.

That amazing silvery blonde hair is in a high ponytail and she's wearing a T-shirt and jeans, but the T-shirt is molded to her body. I can tell by the slight sway to her tits as she steps inside that they are 100% natural and I bet would feel fantastic in my hands.

Fuck. I shake my head again and concentrate.

"I just don't know why we need to hire a bodyguard for me," Joslyn is saying to what I now see is a woman walking in behind her.

That's right. Her mother, Madeline Meyers. Jerico told me she'd be attending this meeting and from those few words, I know that Joslyn isn't here because she wants a bodyguard. Her mom does.

And that means she's probably not a diva, but I'll reserve judgment for now.

"I'm not going to argue with you about this," her mom says as she steps inside and the door swings shut. Madeline sees me standing there and that causes Joslyn to turn my way.

Jesus. She's more beautiful staring at her head on. She looks at me with wide, unblinking eyes and to my horror, her eyes slowly travel down the length of me and then back up again. It's not done with a sexualized appreciation, more like she's stunned by what she sees and can't help but to look closer. When she meets my eyes again, her face flames beet red and her gaze drops to the floor.

I force my attention to her mother and offer her a smile as I hold my hand out. "Mrs. Meyers... I'm Kynan McGrath."

She gives me a brief handshake and looks around. "Pleasure. This is my daughter, Joslyn."

It seems every muscle in my body tightens as I turn her way, because on a physical level, I've never been this attracted to a woman before. Thankfully she's looking at me now with a bland, reserved expression, although there's still a tinge of pink on her cheeks.

I don't offer my hand because I'm actually afraid to touch her for fear of some mystical electrical spark that would snap between us. She doesn't offer her hand either but I give her a nod of acknowledgment.

Turning back to Mrs. Meyers, I suggest, "Let's go into our conference room and we can discuss your concerns about Joslyn's safety."

"There are no concerns," Joslyn murmurs but Mrs. Meyers gives me a tight smile as she ignores her daughter.

I lead them through the lobby, down a short hall, and to a small conference room that has a round table with four chairs. It's a more intimate setting so they'll both feel more comfortable.

As for me, I'm not sure there's anything that could make me comfortable around Joslyn and for a moment, I hate myself for that weakness. In my twenty-six years of living, I've never let a woman affect anything other than my cock. In just the moments since I've met her, my entire body seems to vibrate in awareness of her.

I offer coffee, tea, water, or soda. I would like a few shots of bourbon myself, but that's an impossibility. They both decline and once we're settled at the table with Mrs. Meyers to my left and Joslyn taking the chair directly across from me, I ask a generalized question and wait to see who answers. That tells me who's leading this march.

"Why do you think personal security is needed?"

Joslyn's gaze turns to her mom, who regards me with an aloof sort of professionalism. I don't think she's in "mother" mode at all.

"As Joslyn's act has become more popular here in Vegas, she's started to accrue a fan following. There have been a few concerning incidents and I don't want to take any of them lightly. What might seem like an innocent fascination might turn into a real security threat to my daughter."

I give her an understanding nod. "I'd like more details on what's happened so far to worry you. It will help me determine if we can be of help."

Joslyn's gaze drops down to her lap where her hands are tucked. Mrs. Meyers launches into a litany of events that have occurred from anonymous love letters and gifts to exuberant fans copping a feel when she signs autographs and takes photos after a show. "She keeps getting typed letters from one fan that are just plain creepy," she continues on. "Talks about how he's in love with her but he doesn't have the guts to approach her for a picture or autograph because she'll reject him."

I note a reaction from Joslyn in the form of a heavy eye roll, so I question it. "You don't agree that these are concerning?"

"He didn't say he was afraid I'd reject him," she clarifies to me and gives her mom a stern look for perhaps massaging the words. "He said he didn't want to be a bother."

"Same thing," her mom says with a casual wave her hand. "The fact that he's sent multiple letters all saying the same thing is a clue that he's slightly obsessed with her."

I'd have to agree with Mrs. Meyers on this and it's not a good sign. So I turn back to Joslyn and push at her. "How come you're not concerned with this?"

To my surprise, Joslyn sighs and gives her mom a quick but apologetic smile before turning my way. "It's not that I don't think that stuff's weird, because I do, but it just seems... I don't know... a little overboard to hire security."

"A lot of high-profile people do it," I point out to her.

"You see," she drawls with a frustrated look on that incredibly gorgeous face, "I'm not high profile. I'm just a Vegas act. It seems... a little pretentious to me, is all."

And my attraction to her increases exponentially with those words. She's not a princess or a diva at all. In fact, she seems incredibly grounded for a nineteen-year-old and that shit is sexy to me.

Apparently.

It's not ever happened before... me being attracted to something other than the physical assets.

I push that aside though and turn back to Mrs. Meyers. "Do you want full-time security or just when she's out in public?"

"Full-time," she replies.

"That's going to be expensive," I tell her, knowing that if anything kills this deal it will be the money.

Mrs. Meyers waves me off with a casual flick of her wrist. "I had it written into her contract that they would pay for full-time security upon our request if we wanted it. And I want it, and I want your firm. I realize you and Mr. Jameson are young and new to the game, but you come highly recommended and we want to hire you."

That impresses me—that she's had the foresight to require the casino provide security for her daughter—and I think Joslyn's mom seems to have a really good head on her shoulders. Still, I need the actual client to be okay with it.

Turning my gaze to Joslyn, I tell her, "While we will be as unobtrusive as possible, you need to be the one to approve this. You'll need to follow our instructions when you're out in public and you may have to modify your routines a bit. But I think based on what your mom has told me, that it's warranted."

She regards me a moment, those light blue eyes churning with indecision. She glances at her mom, then back to me as she nibbles on her lip.

Christ... wish that wasn't sexy too.

Finally, she gives me a slight nod. "We can try it out."

And while I should want to steer clear of this woman who seems to affect me on so many levels it's ridiculous, I can't force away the feeling of relief that she's going to hire us.

I am actually looking forward to watching over her.

Chapter 4

Joslyn

Two paces to the front door. I reach out to touch the knob, then jerk my hand back as I reconsider. Turning, I stride away three paces and stop as I tell myself, "Just go for it, Joslyn."

I've been doing this for ten minutes now and I might be certifiably crazy. But I haven't been able to concentrate since *he* arrived at the apartment I share with my mom. He performed what he called a "sweep" once he got here and assured my mom that everything looked secure. He checked out the alarm system that came with the place and pronounced it satisfactory, then immediately stationed himself outside our door in the hallway.

God, he looked amazing, too. Not all buttoned up like yesterday at his office with his tailored suit and short, military-style haircut. He was clean shaven and with that silky British accent that caught me totally off guard when he first spoke, I thought he was quite the dapper business man.

Today though...

Black military-style cargo pants tucked into combat boots that were new and shiny but looked like they could totally stomp some ass and a well-fit black T-shirt with the words Jameson Group in white over the left side of the chest. The T-shirt was short sleeved and molded around impressively huge biceps you couldn't quite appreciate under the tailoring of his suit.

Best of all... yummiest of all, actually... is the two full sleeves of tattoos he has on his arms. I can't help being a sucker for a bad boy, or at least a boy that looks bad. My mom gave them a double-take when she saw them then hardened her jawline in a slightly disapproving look. However, nothing could be said because she'd hired the Jameson Group and because they were so highly recommended by the casino owner where my theater is housed, she wasn't going to let that dissuade her from allowing this man to protect me.

I tried to act casual and disinterested as I sat on the couch with a note pad in front of me and my guitar on my lap. I worked on some new compositions, but I'd peer up through the long layer of hair across my forehead every once in a while. He didn't look at me once, though, other than a brief smile when he walked in.

Then he was gone—sitting just outside the door in the hallway— and I tried to return to my lyrics. My mom made herself a slice of whole wheat avocado toast and pressed one upon me as well. What I really wanted was a bowl of Lucky Charms, but that made me feel juvenile and I didn't want to feel that way.

Not when Kynan McGrath was definitely causing me to have very grown-up, adult feelings.

I pace back toward the door, still undecided. My mom left forty-five minutes ago to do some shopping. It's her thing. She's a fashionista of the highest degree and when she landed me this lucrative Vegas contract, from which I readily agreed to pay her a very nice salary, she began spending her money very seriously. I don't mind, though, because first and foremost, it's her money, but also because she works hard for me and I wouldn't begrudge her anything that rewarded her for it.

Just do it, I tell myself.

Before I can reconsider, I'm snatching the door open and stepping out into the hallway. I didn't startle Kynan but he gives me a worried expression. "What's wrong?"

My mind goes blank for a minute, and I can't for the life of me remember what even led me to open that door. Then I blurt, "I want to play Scrabble."

His chin jerks inward as his eyebrows go up. "Pardon me?"

Pardon me.

Oh my God... swooning here over that British accent.

"Um... yeah," I continue, refusing to lower my gaze over the blatant lie I'm about to tell him. "I'm trying to compose lyrics and I'm stuck.

I've found that playing Scrabble for some reason gets me past the block. I guess it's looking at all those letters and trying to create words from them or something."

His look is dubious but more alarmingly, aloof. "I can't while I'm on duty."

Does that mean he'd play with me when he's off duty?

Scrabble, I mean.

But I can't wait for that. I can't sit around and wonder if he'll ask me out on a Scrabble date, because I'm thinking most likely not. I'm just a job. A client. Nothing more.

In addition, he's older than me. I'm not sure by how much but while he looks young and handsome and fit and muscular and just absolutely perfect in my eyes, he seems a lot older and wiser than I am. What could he possibly want with someone like me?

Normally, this would be the time I'd back off. I'd lose my confidence in myself and beat a hasty retreat. But when he looks at me with those warm brown eyes and I can see all those tattoos in my peripheral vision, I shore up my resolve. "Well, I'm the boss and I say part of your duty is to play Scrabble with me. You can protect me just as well in here as you can out there, right?"

"I was out here," he replies drolly, "because I didn't want to intrude on you. It's not necessarily the better place to be."

"Perfect," I exclaim with a clap of my hands and turn my back on him to walk into the apartment. I don't wait to see if he follows but call out over my shoulder. "Make yourself at home in the kitchen and I'll go get the game."

My heart is pounding as I lift the board game down from a shelf in my closet. I pretty much just deviously calculated a way to put that man within my path so I can pretty much leer at him. How screwed up is that? I've never done that before. Never been so forward. Never reached out for something tangible that I wanted.

And I do want him. I can't explain it because I've never felt it before. It's a palpable, almost mystical feeling, as if I could actually wrap my arms around a misty cloud yet feel its perfection with my heart.

Hey... that would be a great lyric. I set the board game down on my bed and whip my phone out of my pocket. I type that out in my Notes app and save it.

When I return to the kitchen, I've calmed my racing heart a bit but Kynan isn't there. I walk into the living room and find him looking out the large window that gives an amazing view of the Strip in the distance.

He turns to face me and nods toward the furniture. "I'd rather sit in here if you don't mind. So I can see the door?"

I grin at him. "Expecting some crazy guy to come busting in or something?"

Kynan doesn't smile back. "It could happen. It's what crazy obsessed fans do."

That sobers me and my smile slides away.

His face turns cloudy. "I didn't mean to scare you."

"You didn't," I tell him, but he so did. I want to believe my mom is being overly cautious but to hear Kynan validate her concerns has me worried.

"It's fine," he assures me and casually strolls over to one of the guest chairs that faces the front door. He pulls it up close to the coffee table that separates it from the couch. "Let's play."

We're five words into the game and it's his turn when I get up the guts to start a conversation. As he studies his letters with his finger tapping against his chin, I clear my throat and say, "So what's your story? How did you get involved in this type of work?"

His gaze lifts and he stares at me in this way that says he's glad I started a conversation.

At least that's what I think it means. So, I blurt, "I mean... where are you from? How old are you? Are you married?"

The corners of Kynan's mouth curve upward at my last question, and I can tell that for some reason, he's pleased with that level of curiosity. Still, he doesn't satisfy me because he merely says, "I was in the Royal Marines and served in Afghanistan with Jerico Jameson. He just started up this company a few months ago and hired me to work with him."

Hmmm... that sounds sexy and hot but leaves me hanging.

"I'd say you're... twenty-four?" I press.

"Twenty-six," he says and then lays out five tiles to spell out B-O-U-N-C-E vertically from my lame-ass word B-E-A-R.

"And your wife's name?" I ask sweetly, because he's making me work for it and he's enjoying making me work for it.

"No wife," he says as he refills his tile holder thingy.

My mind races to the next level of personal questions I can ask him, but he turns serious again. His eyes are focused and intent. "Your mom was right in hiring a security company for you. You've drawn enough attention in the Vegas area to be considered one of their superstars. You know that, right?"

I'm flattered and frazzled all at once. He clearly researched me, but he also thinks way too highly of me. I don't want to believe those things he saying about me, because I still struggle with confidence in my abilities on a daily basis.

So I deflect by saying something that truly surprises me. "She's not my mom but my stepmom."

Kynan blinks at me in surprise and my face flushes with awful guilt for reducing her down. I hold my hands out. "I didn't mean that in the bad way it sounded. Of course, she's my mom through and through. Raised me since I was six and I love her dearly."

My words trail off and Kynan just watches me. I feel like a bug under a microscope with a hot glaring light just overhead to illuminate the worst of my flaws.

"I'm not sure why I felt the need to distinguish her that way," I murmur as my gaze falls to the board. "It makes me sound like an ungrateful brat."

"It makes it sound like there are times in your life that you need to categorize her," he replies and my head pops up in surprise. "She wears different hats. She's a mother and your business manager. They are two different things and I bet they often conflict."

I nod stupidly, because yes... THAT exactly.

"And I expect," Kynan continues on, "that when she might be failing a bit on the mom side, and perhaps becoming a little overbearing on the manager side—say for example hiring a security firm that you don't believe is necessary—you need to have her be just a stepmom so you can express your anger and frustration a bit."

Again... more nodding with my mouth hanging open.

Kynan smiles at me. "I didn't take what you said to be ungrateful or bratty in any way. I think your relationship with your mom is complex but I've seen the way you look at her and talk to her. I know you love her. You have nothing to prove to me."

Is this guy a security professional or a psychologist, because I think he just boiled down all my frustrations into something that actually sounds acceptable to my conscience?

With a sigh, I sit back on the couch. "I'm not sure when it happened, but at some point, she wasn't satisfied with just managing the business side of my career. Now she wants to control all of me."

"How so?" Kynan asks as he puts his elbows to his knees and clasps his hands together. The game has been forgotten and now we're just conversing.

"She tells me what to eat, what to drink, where to go, where I can't go, how much to exercise, what clothes to wear, and who I can have for friends. I can't go out and have fun because it's too dangerous or I could fall in with the wrong people, and frankly... part of the reason she hired your company was to just add a babysitter on me. She doesn't even want me to have any say-so on the type of jobs I take on. It's like my opinion just doesn't matter."

"You're an adult," Kynan says and the deep timbre of his voice gives me a slight shiver. Acknowledging he doesn't see me as still a teenager, which technically I am. "Why do you let her control you that way?"

"Because she's done so much for me that was good, both for my career and as a mom. She took care of my father when he died a slow cancerous death."

Kynan winces. "I'm sorry. When was that?"

Smiling through the sadness, I murmur. "Almost two years ago. And like I said... when my album didn't do as well as we'd hoped, she landed me this amazing deal here in Vegas. A stepping stone is what she calls it, to bigger and better things."

"Is that what you want? Bigger and better?"

My shrug is slow and without indifference, more of an indication that sometimes I'm not sure I know what I really want. Except for one thing. "I just want to sing. That's all."

Kynan smiles at me and my heart skips a beat. "It's a good priority, Joslyn."

Hearing him say my name makes my skin prickle, or maybe it's the way he's staring at me so intently from across the table. He makes me feel completely stripped and bare, causing me to self-consciously wrap my arms around my stomach.

Not because he makes me feel afraid or threatened, but because he induces what feels like a million fluttering butterflies in my stomach.

Chapter 5

Kynan

I have no business being here. I went off duty over three hours ago and Jayce has watch over Joslyn tonight. But apparently spending eight hours with her today wasn't enough for me, so I stayed on, using the excuse that I wanted to check out the venue where she performs and assess how our security protocol is working during a live show.

Bunch of bullshit but Jayce didn't question it.

Wouldn't have mattered if he had.

Frankly, I can't stand the guy, although I could never quite put my finger on why before tonight. Call it a vibe or a gut instinct, but from the moment Jerico introduced us, I sensed he was bad news. I didn't say anything to Jerico, though, because it wasn't my place. Plus, Jerico felt obligated to Jayce because he saved his life once.

I grudgingly admit that might count for something.

At any rate, tonight I figured out why I don't like him and it's because I've caught him several times openly leering at Joslyn. Never when she's looking though. He puts on the front of a dedicated security professional. When he stands near her, he's alert and watching his surroundings.

But every once in a while, when her attention is elsewhere, his eyes will drop to her arse or her breasts, and I want to rip his head off. I spent all day with her today—playing Scrabble, taking her to the grocery store for Chia seeds which I don't even want to know what that shit is— and otherwise engaged in conversation so perfect that my eight-hour shift was seemingly over in a nanosecond. After just a day with her, I'm feeling all kinds of proprietary and yes, I know that shit is whack.

She's a job.

A client.

I can't be feeling anything for her other than a dedication to my job to protect her life.

My hands ball into fists as I stand beside Jayce just at the edge of the stage, and we watch her final song. She's wearing a black body suit with sparkling crystals sewn all over. Chunks of the unitard are cut out in strategic places, revealing parts of her body.

Right across her breasts.

Her lower back.

Outer thigh.

One entire arm.

Hints of flesh and sexiness as she struts across the stage. The song has a hip-hop vibe to it and her backup dancers are really good. But Joslyn is amazing, particularly performing some of the moves in four-inch stiletto heeled boots in black patent leather.

What I love most about her look tonight though is her hair. It's long, loose, flowing. It seems to have way more volume than normal and I'm not sure how that's accomplished, but when she dances it bounces and sways in almost a mesmerizing fashion. I met her stylist, Michel, tonight when I followed Jayce and Joslyn to the theater inside The Blue Diamond Casino. I would have rather brought her in my vehicle so we could continue to talk, but I was technically off duty and Jayce was on. Besides, I didn't want anyone to even hazard a guess that I might be a little crazy over this girl, especially since it's inappropriate as hell.

I sure as hell don't want anyone to know that half of those thoughts about her are dirty as fuck, because as much as I like her mind and her personality, I like her exterior package a hell of a lot too. Images of me holding her hair while I'm in her from behind threaten to make my cock go rogue, so I think of something else.

Like the way Jayce has a look in his eye right now as he watches her. The kind of look that makes me want to sneak into his apartment tonight and slit his throat.

Leaning in toward him, I say, "She's finishing up. Go and do a sweep of her dressing room."

Jayce startles and looks at me for a moment as if he doesn't understand what I just said. But I am his superior and he's a military man so he knows how to take orders. "Sure thing."

Jayce leaves and I give my attention not to Joslyn, but to the surroundings. My eyes roam the theater, looking for that one crazy who might want to rush the stage. It's happened during a few of her performances before, usually by a drunk, horny teenager. I don't look back at Joslyn now that Jayce is gone as right now it's my full job to protect her.

* * * *

I hang back a few steps while Joslyn and Michel walk toward her dressing room with their arms linked together. As she walked off the stage and straight toward me, she was still smiling and waving to her fans. The minute she was out of their sight, her entire body seemed to almost sag and I started to reach out for her. But then Michel was there, putting an arm around her waist and giving praise for her performance. She looked unsure about his compliments but then her smile returned. It was a clear moment of self-doubt she was having and it surprised me. She's fucking fantastic and I don't understand how she could even have a moment's hesitation in owning that.

It's gone now though. She's all smiles and laughter with Michel as we approach her dressing room. Jayce is standing outside in the classic security guard stance—legs spread, hands clasped together at his lower back and spine ramrod straight.

Michel opens the door and disappears inside. I move to stand on the other side of Jayce but Joslyn touches my arm. "Please come in."

I don't know what to say to that. She wants me in her dressing room. Why? Michel is in there and so is her mother, who chooses to wait there during the performances.

She doesn't wait for me to acknowledge her request but steps over the threshold. I follow her in and shut the door behind me.

Madeline Meyers—dressed in a chic white pantsuit with wide legs— is sitting on the loveseat set against a short wall of the cramped little room. She's got a magazine on her lap, one leg crossed over the other.

Without glancing up, she asks no one in particular, "How did it go?"

Michel responds. "She slayed it, of course. As usual."

"Wonderful," Madeline says and shoots a proud but short smile at Joslyn. She then nods at a large glass filled with a green liquid sitting on the vanity table where Michel styles Joslyn up before a show. "Drink your smoothie."

Joslyn wrinkles her nose but picks the glass up. I'm not crazy about vegetables to begin with—corn and maybe potatoes are okay—so I have a sympathy gag reflex when she takes a large swallow, struggling to get it down.

Madeline goes back to reading her magazine.

Joslyn watchers her mom a moment, perhaps wondering what would happen if she dumped the drink in the garbage. The expression on her face is definitely calculating, like she's mentally weighing odds about something.

She seems to come to a decision, if the resolved look in her eyes is any indication, and she takes another large swallow of the drink. Turning her back to Michel, she says, "Unzip me."

My entire body goes taut, as I realize she's going to undress in front of me. Madeline pays no attention and Michel doesn't think twice. He steps up and takes the zipper at the top of her neck, dragging it slowly down until it stops just above the crack of her butt. I try not to look—honestly, I do—but the bare skin being revealed is too irresistible and the fact I don't see a scrap of lace or silk at the bottom tells me she's not wearing panties under that skintight suit.

Fuck.

Joslyn looks at me, one corner of her mouth lifting up as she breezes by me to a three-panel privacy screen in the corner. She disappears behind it and I hear the sound of her glass being set down upon something. Michel goes to the vanity and busies himself organizing, and Madeline is absorbed in her magazine.

From the corner of my eye, the black, sparkly outfit is tossed over the top of the screen, and my cock actually thumps from the knowledge the Joslyn is completely naked on the other side.

"Michel," she says in a blasé voice. "Let's go out dancing tonight."

At this, Madeline's head pops up. She looks at Michel, who freezes in place, looking at Madeline through the reflection of the vanity mirror. Dropping her gaze to her magazine, she says in a stern voice, "That's not a good idea."

Michel ducks his head and pretends he's ignoring everything, but his body tenses. I get the feeling he's witnessed some awkward conversations between mother and daughter over the last several months.

"It's a great idea," Joslyn says in a pleasant voice.

Madeline's eyes raise and pin hard against the privacy screen, as if she could bore holes through it to reach her daughter. "I don't want you—"

"To what?" Joslyn cuts in and her head pops out from the side of the screen. Her shoulders are bare and I wonder if she had time to put on panties yet. Her expression is defensive. "Don't want me partying? Making a bad name for myself? Hanging out with the wrong people? Embarrassing you? Myself? Tanking my career?"

I blink in surprise at the vehemence in her voice. All indications so far lead me to believe that Joslyn definitely defers to her mother in most things. Clearly, this is an age-old argument between the two of them.

Madeline softens her voice to a placating tone. "I don't want you to be in danger."

Joslyn's face also goes soft and her voice sweetens. "You don't have to worry about that. I now have a bodyguard."

I get a side-eyed glance from Joslyn and I have to bite the inside of my cheek to keep from laughing.

"I'm not paying them to babysit you while you party," Madeline replies tightly.

"First," Joslyn says with heat returning to her voice, "I don't party. But I do like to dance. And second, the casino is paying for Jameson Group, not you."

Madeline opens her mouth but I find myself intervening in a place I should absolutely keep my fucking mouth shut. "Ma'am... it's part of our job. To watch Joslyn wherever she goes, twenty-four hours a day. It's something we routinely do... attending social events with our clients for their protection."

I have no clue if this is true. This is my first personal security detail but we have it set up for three separate shifts in a twenty-four-hour period, which includes overnight protection. So I'm going to assume my job is to watch over Joslyn wherever she may be.

Or rather, it's Jameson's job and my job if I'm on duty.

Madeline glares at me, her jaw locked tight, then lets her gaze fall back down to the magazine. She tries to go for easygoing but her voice is clipped and offended. "Fine. Have a good time and be careful."

"I will," Joslyn says, her voice truly gentling so that her mom won't worry.

Madeline doesn't acknowledge her at all and Joslyn sighs as she disappears behind the privacy screen once again.

Chapter 6

Joslyn

I'm an excellent dancer. Singing is definitely where my passion lies, but I'm glad I sing stuff that is conducive to dancing. Anyone who is anyone at the top of the pop charts has to be able to entertain the masses with what's below their shoulders. So my mom made sure to put me in dance when I was a kid to hone the natural talent I already possessed.

When I'm on stage, it's different. It's a job and perfection is my goal. Those moves are choreographed, rehearsed, and then drilled into my muscle memory show after show. I can perform without much thought.

Here on the dance floor, the liberating freedom to move to the beat the way I want to almost makes me giddy.

Also, it might have something to do with the fact that Kynan's watching me.

I'm so glad he's not being obvious in his security duty to me. While both he and Jayce are dressed the same in the black cargo utilities, tight T-shirts with the Jameson logo, and ass-stomping boots, they're doing their best to blend. Jayce is on an open, upper dance floor balcony, with his forearms casually resting on the top rail that surrounds it. I've glanced up at him a few times and each time, he's just slowly glancing around the club, looking for potential danger.

I'm happily surprised that Kynan came, as it was my deep hope that he would. He's off duty technically but he's still watching things carefully from the bar area. He's got an arm propped on the top and is nursing a club soda. While he too looks around, keeping an alert eye on my surroundings, I have several times caught him just watching me.

Dance.

Rotate my hips.

Stretch my arms high above my head so my halter top rides up and exposes my stomach.

My cheeks heat a little as I realize I'm actually putting on a show just for him.

But so be it. I can't deny the intense attraction I have to him, nor can I deny that talking to him and hanging out with him today has been the most genuinely spent time that I've had in ages. It was actually refreshing.

Michel grins at me as he moves to the same beat as I am. He's a pretty damn good dancer too and he's putting on a show of his own for one of the bouncers. A big burly guy that has had his eye right back on Michel. He'll probably get lucky tonight, but that's all Michel will be interested in. Since he had his heart broken by his first love, he's not willing to put it back out there again to get stomped on.

That makes me so sad, but what do I really know about it? I've never been in love before. I dated in high school and while touring the year my album came out. I lost my virginity to one of my backup dancers about six months ago and it's part of the reason my mom doesn't fully trust me. She caught him sneaking out of my bedroom that night, which was a terribly awkward situation.

I gyrate my hips, almost lewdly, and glance back over at Kynan. It's one of the times he's looking directly at me and his stare is intense. I'm not purposely trying to tease him and I'm not leading him on. I totally want him for reasons I still can't fathom outside of his unholy attractiveness. I've never been this bowled over by a guy before. But I feel compelled to make him watch me and I'm not going to apologize for it, or for the hunger that I think I see glittering in his eyes.

Michel moves in close to me, puts his mouth by my ear, and has to speak a bit loudly to be heard over the music. "You're so bad."

I jerk my chin in and look at him with pure innocence. "What do you mean?"

"You're going to get yourself fucked up against a wall in the back alley if you don't quit dancing that way in front of tall, blond, and British," he replies.

I roll my eyes and pretend that I have no clue what he's talking about, all the while wondering what that would be like. Sadly, my one experience with sex was not overly thrilling. Still, I'm not stupid enough to believe that's the way it always is. In fact, I'd bet my contract here in Vegas that Kynan would be a phenomenal lover.

A small shiver runs up my spine. I glance at him again and I'm disappointed to find Jayce at his side. He's listening intently to something that Kynan says, then nods and pulls his phone out of his pocket. He dials someone and puts it up to his ear, pivoting away from Kynan and walking to the exit doors.

"Girlfriend," Michel calls in my ear again and I'm startled. I give him my attention while we dance in place. "I'm making my move. It's getting late and if I'm going to get that bouncer to take me home when the club closes, I'm going to need to start some serious face-to-face flirting with him."

Grinning, I put my hands to Michel's shoulders and go up on tiptoes to feather a kiss on his cheek. "Good luck and thank you for being such a good friend to me. I don't know what I'd do without you."

"I had fun tonight," he says. "Let's do this on all your nights off."

"Agreed," I say with a laugh and I finish out the song on the dance floor while Michel engages himself in conversation with the bouncer.

When a new beat starts, I turn toward the bar and find Kynan watching me again. He jerks his chin in an indication he wants to talk to me and so I head his way. I had a bottled water resting on the bar near his club soda and I grab it when I reach him.

"What's up?" I ask him.

"Jayce's shift is almost up," he says. "I told him I'd get you and Michel home and he's having the next guy on duty just head over to your house."

"Well, Michel has his own ride home," I say as I turn to look at him over my shoulder. When I look back to Kynan, I see him staring at Michel and the big bouncer with a grin.

His eyes come back to mine, filled with amusement. "Looks like it's just you and me then."

The words were in jest, but they pack a punch.

Just me and him.

Together.

Alone.

Late at night.

I'm not sure what the expression on my face says, or if it reveals exactly what's bouncing around in my brain, but the smile slides off Kynan's face. In this moment, I know he can read me very clearly.

A tiny muscle tightens at the corner of his jaw and his eyes move over my face, almost as if he's trying to find something other than what he suspects I'm thinking.

Disappointed, because I can think of nothing else and it must show, Kynan looks away from me and back across the club to where Michel is standing. When he looks back to me, his face is impassive and his voice bland. "You sure Michel doesn't need a ride?"

I shake my head. "He's going to stay here and he can always Uber home if need be."

"Are you ready to leave?" he asks me. "Or do you want to dance some more?"

I want to dance some more. With him. Slow and close. "I'm ready to go. Let me just go tell Michel good-bye."

Crossing the dance floor, I weave my way in and out of gyrating bodies. When I reach Michel—who is in heavy duty flirtation mode with the bouncer—I tap him on the shoulder. He turns with an annoyed expression on his face which melts away when he sees it's me.

"Kynan is taking me home," I tell him.

Michel smirks at me. "Don't do anything I wouldn't do."

Rolling my eyes, I tell him, "That's not helpful at all since you would do almost anything and everything."

Michel gives a sideways glance at the bouncer, who is listening carefully to our exchange, and runs his eyes up and down. "Girl, you know that's true."

The corners of the bouncer's mouth curve up in a sly way as he realizes he's getting laid tonight.

Michel and I air kiss each other's cheeks good-bye and I turn to make my way back across the dance floor to Kynan. I get no more than three steps before a hand is grabbing my upper arm and I'm being whipped around so fast my head spins. Then I'm pulled hard into a man's body and a hand goes to my ass.

Brushing my hair out of my eyes, I don't even have the time to see who my aggressor is or even be offended before the guy just disappears. It takes me a moment to realize he's flat on his back in the middle of the dance floor with Kynan crouched over him. One hand is wrapped around the front of the guy's throat and the other is just casually loose near his hip. He doesn't seem to be expending any energy whatsoever but the guy on the floor is clawing at Kynan with both hands and writhing around as his face turns purple.

Then Kynan lets him go and stands up.

It all happens so fast, the bouncer nearest us—Michel's date tonight—doesn't even have a chance to move. Kynan doesn't give the man who grabbed me another look nor does he care about all the people gawking at us.

He takes me by the elbow and steers me across the dance floor. People scramble to get out of the way of the huge man that just laid that jerk out in about a nanosecond without breaking a sweat.

Kynan's strides are long so I have to trot to stay at pace with him. In moments I'm outside of the club and we're making our way across the parking lot. I dare a glance up at him and he looks incredibly pissed.

When we reach his vehicle—a black Suburban with tinted windows—he lets me go. "Are you hurt?"

I shake my head rapidly and venture a question of my own. "Are you mad at me?"

"Fuck no," he growls and then rubs the back of his neck in what seems to be frustration. "I just... lost my shit in there when he grabbed you like that. I could have fucking killed him."

I'm not sure what meaning he places behind his actions, but I know the reaction of my body to them. He got mad on a personal level that someone touched me and that does something incredibly disturbing to my body. My lower belly tingles, a cramp hits me between the legs, and I feel a rush of wetness against my panties. I squeeze my legs together and that makes the ache worse.

I groan and Kynan's eyes snap to me. "What?"

"Nothing," I mutter.

"Are you sure you're not hurt?" he demands, his head swinging back to the club and I can tell he's considering going back in there to finish the job.

"I'm fine," I assure him, reaching out a hand to touch his arm.

Kynan's body locks tight and his gaze swings back to me before descending to look at me touching him. I snatch my hand back, feeling as if I've been burned not by the touch but by some untold condemnation from him. He doesn't like me touching him.

His expression is troubled for a moment—as if I've crossed a line—then goes blank. Leaning past me, he opens the passenger door and holds it open for me to get in. "Let's get you home."

"Okay," I murmur, unsure of what the hell just happened but with a sneaking suspicion that my attraction to Kynan may not be reciprocated after all.

Chapter 7

Kynan

I don't let Joslyn mesmerize me too much. I'm on duty and she's on stage, and while she's captivating in a way I've never known, I am more interested right now in making sure she's safe. I've changed the shift schedule to just two twelve-hour shifts. Jayce was moved to cover 6AM to 6PM and I cover the other 12 hours. I chose the evening shift so I could watch over Joslyn when she's at her most vulnerable—which is anywhere away from the apartment but most importantly when she's performing.

Selfishly, I also chose this shift because after her shows or the nights she has off, we come back to the apartment and hang out. I'm still on duty and most properly, I should probably be standing outside the door in the hallway, but sitting in the living room with her is just as good. I have line of sight of the door, a security system someone would have to bust through, and a 9mm gun on my hip.

We've taken to playing board games, which usually ends up being about 90 percent talking with each other and only about 10 percent of gameplay. The first time Madeline witnessed this, she gave me a funny look. Not quite disapproving but definitely uneasy with the way Joslyn and I were sitting on opposite sides of the table as we discussed our favorite classic rock songs. Joslyn has an amazing variety of music that she listens to, which is something we have in common.

I don't care what Madeline thinks. I'm protecting her daughter and fulfilling my secret crush at the same time. I could no more stay away from Joslyn out in that hallway than I could decide to give up oxygen. In just a little over a week, she's become that important to me.

Or I've become that obsessed with her.

My gaze sweeps the audience, cuts to Joslyn for just a minute as she croons a love song while sitting on a stool center stage with a spotlight illuminating all of that gorgeous silvery hair.

Back to the audience for only a moment as I feel someone step up beside me at the edge of the stage. I twist my neck and see Jerico standing there. He's dressed in a business suit and lifts his chin in greeting.

"You're back," I say as my gaze returns to the crowd.

"Got in a few hours ago but thought I'd come catch our first personal client's show," he explains to me. "Also wanted to meet her mother."

"She's in Joslyn's dressing room," I tell him.

"Yeah... already been there and introduced myself." Jerico slips his hands casually into his pockets and adds, "She's an um... intense woman."

"She's dedicated to Joslyn's career," I mutter, wondering sometimes what's more important to her. Being a mother or being a manager.

My eyes slide to Joslyn. It's something she struggles with understanding as well. Late at night and long after Madeline retires, Joslyn stays up and keeps me company until the wee hours of the morning before I have to leave. We'll push the board game aside. She settles back onto the couch while I stay perched on the edge of the guest chair, always facing the front door. Over the last four evenings I've been with her, we've probably wracked up a good twenty hours of one-on-one conversation.

Let me tell you... you can learn a lot about a person in that amount of time.

On the flip side, I opened up to her, which is incredibly odd. I'm not overly close with my family but there's no drama there. I spend most of my time telling her about my military service, and although I know it distresses her to learn some of the harrowing things that have happened to me, I can't seem to stop myself from sharing. She's the only person in this world that knows I almost pissed my pants one night when I was out on a patrol and a grenade got tossed over my head, landing just about twenty feet from me. It landed in the middle of some of my closest friends, killing three of them and throwing me several feet away from the force of the explosion.

When I told her that story, her eyes got a little misty and she made a move to get off the couch.

To come to me.

I gave a slight shake of my head, not because I didn't want her touch or comfort, but because I was afraid I wanted it too much.

"So I was thinking about hitting a strip club after the show," Jerico says and it startles me because I was so lost in my memories.

"Huh?" I ask, snapping my gaze from Joslyn to him.

"Strip club," he reiterates. "I'll get someone to come cover the rest of your shift. I want to get drunk tonight, ogle some tits, and then hopefully take a beauty home to fuck. And you've always been up for that type of fun, so let's do it. We've been working our asses off and deserve it."

Yeah, I love a good titty bar. Love good pussy too.

My eyes drift back to Joslyn and I know that I would have better with her.

"No, thanks," I tell him and then straighten my spine a little more, letting my attention turn to the crowd again.

Doing my job.

"You need to cut that shit out right now," Jerico growls and I turn to face him.

"What do you mean?"

Jerico's eyes cut to Joslyn out on stage and he merely nods at her. "I can see it. You might be hiding it from everyone else but not from me. You can't get involved with her."

"I'm not," I grit out.

"She's a job," he tells me pointedly. As if I didn't understand what he had just said.

"I get that."

His expression turns hard. "She's too young anyway."

Not really. "I know."

But he is right. I can't get involved with her.

My ears train onto the sound of her voice, which is just as good as looking at her. The timbre and the huskiness drive deep into me. I get joy listening to the raucous applause after every song she finishes. That moment on her face after her last number when she realizes she killed it out there and can breathe easy again.

Yeah, even her fucking insecurities are a turn-on to me.

But I can't have her. Someone can't shine that bright and not be noticed. I know when that happens, Vegas will not be big enough to contain her.

A sense of loss hits me deep in my gut, and I wonder how I can miss something that I never even had.

"Everything set for your trip to Montana?"

His abrupt change of subject relieves me. "Yeah. It's all good."

Joslyn and I leave in a few days for her charity concert event. We'll be in Cunningham Falls for two nights as she wanted to relax a little and see some local friends.

"How many men are you taking?" he asks me.

I turn and regard Jerico curiously, wondering if he's going to be this up in my business on every single case I handle. "Just me and Jayce. It's a very small event and the sheriff there seems to have pretty tight security protocols in place. There is a high tourist population in the summer months so there will be a lot of people to watch, but between the sheriff's department and Jayce and me sticking close to her, she'll be fully covered."

"Is her mother going?" he asks. "Does she need some protection?"

I shake my head. "She's going to New York on a shopping trip but I think it's in protest."

"How do you mean?"

I give him a quick glance and turn back to the stage. "Madeline didn't want Joslyn to take this job. It interfered with a big deal she was putting together and it pissed her off."

"And you know that how?" he asks with a raised eyebrow.

My voice is too damn tight and defensive when I reply, "Because Madeline told me. She asked me to convince Joslyn not to do the concert because of security concerns, but I couldn't do it. It would be lying."

That was a completely awkward conversation two days ago. Madeline was waiting for me out in the hallway when I came on duty. After Jayce left, she told me point blank that she had a better deal for Joslyn just there for the taking if she'd forgo the Cunningham Falls concert. She didn't think I had any sway over her daughter, which meant she wasn't as observant of us as I had surmised, but rather wanted me to come up with some bogus security concerns. I apologized profusely because I just couldn't do it. We'd sent a guy to Cunningham Falls to scope it out and meet with Sheriff Hull to ensure Joslyn's safety. It would be tight and well-run, so I had no qualms about her going.

Moreover, I'm glad I could deny Madeline because this concert was important to Joslyn on an incredibly personal level. I wasn't about to dash her dreams to participate in this as a means to connect with her father's spirit wherever it may be.

"She wasn't happy I wouldn't go to bat for her," I tell Jerico, because I need to disclose to him that I pissed her off. "She tried to remind me she was the client, and not Joslyn, but sorry, mate... I don't agree with it and wasn't about to cow to her."

"Tread careful," Jerico warns. "Because Madeline Meyers is the client in that she controls everything. If she wants to fire us, she can easily and hire someone else. Don't make it easy for her to do so."

That makes me feel like shit. That I'd put Jerico's business in jeopardy, and yet, I can't be fully abashed.

"The concert has deep personal meaning for Joslyn," I tell him, knowing that it does nothing but reveal that I know Joslyn better than I have a right to and everything he suspects about me is true.

Jerico stares at me with worry in his expression.

I dig my grave deeper as I continue to defend Joslyn. "I'm just saying... she told me about her dad dying of cancer and this is going to benefit a memorial wing of the hospital named after him. He was a beloved town doctor. I guess I can't understand how her mother doesn't get that. Or how she thinks something else should be more important."

"She's a business manager as much as a mom," Jerico says in a low tone. "Her job is to focus on career, money, and opportunity."

Funny. I thought her job was first and foremost to be a mother, but apparently not. I hold my tongue, though, as I've painted myself in a bad enough light with Jerico already.

Jerico places a hand on my shoulder and I'm forced to give him my attention. "Joslyn is business, not pleasure."

I shrug his hand off but lean in closer to him so he can hear me clearly. "If you don't trust me to do the job, then by all means... put someone else on it."

Jerico stares at me a moment before replying, "I trust you."

"Then let me do my job." I turn away from him and look back out over the crowd. Joslyn has two more songs to go and then we'll be able to wrap things up for the night.

"I'm headed out," Jerico says and I throw a hand up in

acknowledgment.

He leaves me with one last pearl of wisdom though. "She's not going to be in Vegas long. You know that, right?"

I don't reply but watch Joslyn strut around on the stage, having moved to a high energy pop song with a slight techno beat to it.

"Her trajectory is upward," Jerico continues on and I just wish he'd shut the fuck up. "It will take her away from here. Mark my word."

He's right, of course, and I hate him for it.

So all I can say is, "I know, and that's good. She deserves it."

Chapter 8

Joslyn

"Are you sure you don't need me to stick around?" Michel asks as I change out of my costume. After a show, nothing feels better than a pair of sweat pants and a T-shirt after wearing such uncomfortable clothing.

Well, a shower is better, but there isn't one in my dressing room so that has to wait for when I get home.

Still, Michel normally brushes out my hair, displacing the tangle of teased poufs and hair product, as well as my thick stage makeup.

"I'm good," I tell him as I pull my T-shirt down to my hips and come out from behind the screen. My mother wasn't here after the show, which is highly unusual, and she didn't even leave me a nasty kale smoothie to drink. I think I'll ask Kynan to run me through a McDonald's on the way home. I'd kill for some of their french fries.

Right now, he's standing just outside my dressing room door, patiently waiting for me to get back into my street clothes. He stopped coming in here after that first time I invited him, which amuses me somewhat. Once we get to the apartment, we easily lapse into friendly conversation, teasing, and secret sharing. But here at the venue, he's all business.

Which is hot.

"Okay, I'm out of here," Michel says before pressing a kiss to my cheek. "See you tomorrow."

"Have fun," I call out to him as he opens the door to leave.

"You know it," he chirps back at me. Seems that the bouncer he met the night we went out is intriguing Michel in a way that no man has in a long time. They've seen each other almost every night since.

I get a brief glimpse of Kynan standing outside and smile to myself as I sit down at the vanity table. The mirror is surrounded by round, frosted bulbs that reflect back to me a woman that looks nothing like the real Joslyn Meyers. My makeup is heavy, my hair outrageously wild, and my lips shiny with thick gloss.

I wrinkle my nose and grab a few makeup removal towelettes from a box on the table. I start wiping the gunk off and then dab oil across the tops of my eyelids to free the heavy and incredibly sticky false eyelashes. I dump them in the trash beside me and pull out some more wipes to remove the rest of the eye makeup.

Someone gives a sharp rap to my door and I call, "Come in," thinking it's Kynan.

Instead, I see my mom poke her head in the door through the reflection of the vanity mirror. "You dressed?" she asks.

"Yeah," I reply and she pushes the door wide open to step inside. Behind follows a man that I've never met before. He closes the door after they cross the threshold.

I turn halfway in my chair, putting one arm around the back to look at them straight on.

"Joslyn," my mom says in a gracious voice with an underlying vibration of excitement. "I want to introduce to you Ian McMichaels."

My eyes flare wide. I recognize him now that I know his name and I pop off my chair to face him fully.

He's of average height and looks, with reddish blond hair that is longish but styled. His eyes are green and his face ruddy, covered in freckles and Irish genealogy. If I remember correctly, he's in his early forties but he looks younger than that.

Stepping past my mother, he holds his hand out to me. "It's a pleasure to meet you, Joslyn."

Unfortunately, I'm rendered a bit speechless by the fact that the most sought-after entertainment agent is standing in my dressing room. He represents six of the top ten actors and actresses in Hollywood and has secured amazing deals with major record labels for his signing stars. I manage a quick swipe of my suddenly sweaty hand and hold it out to him.

We shake and a quick glance to my mom shows her watching us with a nervous expression on her face. She waits for me to say something, and when I don't, she rushes in to fill the silence.

"Joslyn... Mr. McMichaels flew in from L.A. to catch your show tonight," my mother says exuberantly. I realize that this is not a surprise to my mom the way it is to me. She must have set this up somehow but didn't tell me, and I'm grateful for it. The pressure of knowing he was in the audience would have put my stomach in knots, sort of the way it's starting to do now that he's here in my dressing room.

"You were amazing," Ian says as he releases my hand and gives me a genial smile. "Your mom was going to bring you to L.A. to meet me, but I understand you had a charity concert that conflicted."

I shoot my mom a quick glance, now understanding why she was so upset that I took the concert. No one would miss a meeting with this man, who has paved the way to gold for so many superstars today. Still, even if I had known that was the opportunity awaiting me, I would have chosen the concert without an ounce of hesitation. I can't even imagine what my mother had to do to get Ian McMichaels here to Vegas to watch me.

"Madeline," Ian says as he looks at me. I find it weird he's addressing my mother without his eyes leaving my face. "Would you give me and Joslyn a minute alone?"

My nerves fire and my stomach flips. My mom just beams him a smile and says, "Of course."

Before I can say anything—which would be my first words of this meeting—my mom is gone and the door is shut.

I turn my attention back to Ian, who is still smiling at me genially with his hands clasped before him. I swallow hard, trying to think of something witty to say, but nothing comes.

Ian takes a step toward me. "Your vocals are perfection and you have incredible dance skills."

Wow... Ian McMichaels thinks I have real talent.

He takes another step, then another, veering around me. He walks around the back of me and I force myself not to turn with him so that I can see what he's doing. I imagine he's checking me out from the back side, which makes me feel a little icky, but I don't dwell on it.

It's Ian McMichaels.

When he comes around my other side, he stops so that I have to turn to face him. I feel incredibly intimidated. His eyes bore into mine and the smile is gone. "But you lack confidence and it shows through like a bright spotlight. I think you have enough talent we could develop you into something worthy of the entertainment industry, but the key word here is 'develop.' You're going to have to work harder than ever before, and you're going to have to do exactly as I say. If you want to make it big, you're going to have to let go of this two-bit act you've got going here and totally change the way you comport yourself or you'll get eaten alive. Am I clear?"

I can feel myself shrinking, what confidence I did have slowly ebbing away with each word. He sees it too and looks disappointed. I manage to straighten and lift my chin, and that delights him. His eyes sparkle and a corner of his mouth lifts. "Good," he praises me. "I see you understand what I mean. The question is, are you ready to work for it?"

I swallow again, and finally manage to find my voice. "I'm sorry... work for what?"

"The opportunities I will bring your way as your agent," he replies smoothly.

"My agent?" I say with surprise. Ian McMichaels wants to represent me?

His smile breaks wide and he chuckles. "I'll handle the details with your mother."

Taking my hand in his, he brings it up to his mouth and brushes his lips over my knuckles. My urge is to pull my hand away and I think he knows it, because he holds on tight and lets his mouth linger there while his eyes hold mine in challenge.

Finally, he lets go and pivots away from me. Without another word, he walks out the door. I'm left standing there, stunned over what just happened and having conflicted feelings about it. Before I can process them, though, the door opens up and my mom slips back inside.

She clasps her hands tight over her chest, trying to hold in a smile that she just can't contain. It breaks, washes over her face and she squeals in excitement.

Then she lunges forward and has her arms around me, hugging me tight. "He wants to sign you, Jos. All our dreams are going to come true."

I try to embrace her back, but I'm too slow witted and she's releasing me anyway. She starts backing toward the door and blows me a kiss. "I'm going to go get a late meal with Ian so we can talk details. I'll tell you all about it later."

I just stare at her and I'm not sure what my expression holds, but it causes her smile to slide. "Aren't you excited?"

I get no opportunity to assure her I am because she's advancing back on me. Her eyes heat and her lips press into a flat line. She puts her hands on my shoulders, squeezes, and puts her face in mine. "You do realize he only represents A-list stars, right? I'm sure you can only imagine what I've gone through to get him here to see you, right? You need to sign with him, Joslyn, and you can't hesitate on this."

"I will," I assure her, bringing my hands up to wrap around her wrists. I give her an affectionate squeeze. "I'll do what you think is best. I'm just overwhelmed."

Her face softens and she smiles at me again. "Good. Because you know that I only want what's best for you. Right?"

I nod, smiling back at her with reassurance.

She stares at me, her eyes roaming over my face for perhaps any evidence of a lie within my promise. Satisfied, she kisses me on my cheek before turning gracefully to the door.

"Mom," I say to get her attention.

She turns back to face me. "Yes, sweetheart?"

"Why don't you come with us to Cunningham Falls?" I ask her with hope blooming in my chest. I want her with me when we celebrate Dad and what he meant to his community.

"Honey," she replies with her eyebrows drawing inward as if she doesn't understand my question. "You know I'm going to New York."

Yes, a shopping trip that she had planned and booked the day I told her I was doing the concert. I thought she was doing it to punish me for agreeing to the concert and supposedly ruining a meeting she was trying to set up with Ian. But that's all water under the bridge now.

"It's a charity benefit," I remind her. "They're going to open a new wing of the hospital named after him."

I don't have to clarify who "him" is.

That would be my dad, who was a doctor in Cunningham Falls. But not just any doctor. He was the small-town doc who would come to your house if you were too sick to get out of bed. He treated those who couldn't afford medical care for free, or he'd accept a bucket of huckleberries in return. He was beloved by everyone, most of all me.

My mom's eyes glisten with welling tears and her voice is small. "It's just too painful for me to go back, Jos. I hope you understand."

She doesn't give me a chance to figure out whether or not I understand, because she's spinning away and breezing out the door.

I blink in surprise, stunned she'd just leave me in the middle of such an important conversation. We're talking about my dad... her husband. He died almost two years ago. It was about six months after my album dropped and we had all figured out that it wasn't going to perform well. I guess the downside to going with a small label with no real marketing power.

Still, through it all, my father always maintained I was going to be a superstar one day. My mom agreed with him, and I know that's why she works so hard for me. Sometimes I think she blames herself for helping me secure that deal with the label. She sees the failure of the album as her failure, whereas I just see it as a learning lesson. Through all of it, my father was our biggest supporter. He even made my mom promise on his deathbed that she would stick by my side and help me achieve my dreams.

She never hesitated because she loved him and me, and as he was dying, she would have promised him the world.

And yet, she can't go back to celebrate the memory of such a man.

It makes no sense to me, and she won't even try to explain her feelings on the matter.

Once again, my dressing room door opens but this time it's Kynan stepping in. He takes one look at me and his expression darkens. "What happened?"

I force a big smile on my face. "Um... great news. That man was the most sought-after talent agent there is and he wants to sign me."

Kynan doesn't smile back. He doesn't congratulate. He merely questions me. "Then how come you look upset?"

"I'm not—"

"You are," he says over me. "What's wrong?"

I shrug but then spill my guts. "I thought maybe my mom would come to Cunningham Falls with us, but she still wants to go to New York for her shopping trip."

"Maybe it's too hard on her to go back," he suggests.

I nod. "That's what she said."

"Give her the benefit of the doubt," he tells me.

I nod again.

Of course I will. I could never question her love for my father. Not when I watched how she took care of him as he died. I need to accept that the way she grieves or honors his memory is not necessarily the way I would.

Chapter 9

Kynan

Joslyn became a different person once we loaded up into the rental SUV and left the airport. The drive into Cunningham Falls only takes about twenty minutes and a good chunk of that time I spent watching Joslyn through the rear-view mirror. She sat in the rear passenger seat behind Jayce. Her forearm was propped just below the window and her forehead rested against the glass. She stared dreamily out at the passing scenery, a tender smile on her face. Her body appeared loose, her posture relaxed, and I'd never seen her so at peace before.

It became glaringly apparent to me in witnessing this transformation that Joslyn bore a lot of stress in her day-to-day life in Vegas.

But now she's never looked more beautiful, with the late afternoon sun bathing her face in a golden glow and her blue eyes glittering with a recognition of something very personal to her.

I've learned a lot about Joslyn, and in turn have learned about her hometown of Cunningham Falls. It's small, boasting just over six thousand permanent residents, although that number swells during tourist seasons. Cunningham Falls sits at the bottom of Whitetail Mountain, which is renowned for its skiing.

Joslyn told me just last night after her show as we were driving home that when she lived here, she couldn't wait to get out and explore the big world, and now that she's been gone, she can't wait to get back to the quiet.

As we enter the small town with streets bordered by unique and trendy-looking shops, Joslyn starts narrating the trip for Jayce and me.

"You can see the resort on top of Whitetail Mountain," she says as her head pops up in between the front seats and she points out the front window. She had to take her seatbelt off to do so but I'm driving about 15 miles per hours so she's safe enough. Besides, I doubt she'd sit back if I told her to. "Oh, and there's Ed's Diner. We have to eat breakfast there tomorrow. Best huckleberry pancakes."

She tells us about the coffee shop, Drips and Sips, and how they have the best lattes. I grimace because that shit is just nasty, but I let her keep talking.

I have to admit, the scenery is stunning. Cunningham Falls sits in the basin of Glacier National Park in the northern Rocky Mountains. Even in the height of summer, the top of the mountains are still tipped with a bit of snow, giving it a postcard picture quality in the dying sunlight of later afternoon.

"Stop," Joslyn squeals and I almost have a heart attack. She points at something out the side window. "We need to stop for ice cream."

I note the little store named Sweet Scoops as Joslyn puts her hand on my shoulder and shakes me. "Stop, please."

Jayce makes a sound deep in his throat and I turn to look at him. He's got a smirk on his face and he's shaking his head, making it clear he thinks this is juvenile. Joslyn doesn't notice as she's now got her face almost pressed into the window glass as she looks at the ice cream shop.

Without hesitation, I pull into an empty spot just one store down. When I put it in park, I feel the weight of Jayce's stare. As Joslyn scrambles out of the SUV, I glare at him. "She's the client. She gets to stop where she wants."

"Of course she does," he mutters and slouches down into his seat. "I'll just wait here."

"Suit yourself," I tell him and exit the vehicle.

While I seriously doubt danger is lurking inside, I trot down the sidewalk to catch up to Joslyn, reaching her just as she opens the door. Her neck twists and she shoots me a blinding smile over her shoulder. "Just wait until you taste the huckleberry ice cream."

"What is it with huckleberries?" I ask her curiously as we step into the shop. It smells heavenly—like vanilla custard with the hint of something tart layered just underneath.

"They're only the best berry ever," she replies enthusiastically as she takes a spot at the end of the line. The place is packed and every seat seems to be taken. "My dad and I would pick them every summer. They grow all over the place here. And Mom makes a great huckleberry pie."

Chuckling, I tell her, "Then I can't wait to try it while I'm here."

Joslyn orders three cones with double scoops of huckleberry ice cream and pays the young girl behind the register. I carry Jayce's out to him, wondering if he'll be put out he has to accept or grateful that Joslyn is a sweet woman who thinks of others.

* * * *

I walk the interior of Joslyn's suite at the Whitetail Mountain Ski Resort. It's just two rooms but it's a lot of space. There's a large living area with a u-shaped couch, a small four-chaired dining table and a desk. The bedroom is set to the side and has double doors leading into it.

Jayce and I are sharing a room that's connected off the other side of the living room and I instructed Joslyn she needed to keep that door unlocked at all times. We would not use it unless there was an emergency, but I need easy access to her if something happens.

Both the living area and bedroom have sliding glass doors that lead out onto a large balcony that overlooks the ski slopes and the town of Cunningham Falls below. It's secure enough and no one could breach this suite from the balcony, as it's independently set apart from the balconies to the left and right. They're also staggered so it would be difficult for someone to drop down from above or jump up from below. Not that Joslyn needs that level of protection. Again, the chances of some random stalker trying to sneak into her room by scaling the outside of the building perched on the edge of a mountain roughly equals my chances of winning the lottery.

Still, it's good practice for me to always assess situations. Never know if I might be protecting someone in the future that would attract a more determined type of criminal.

I walk back to the balcony. Sliding the door open, I step outside and rest my forearms on the thick wooden beam that makes up the top of the rustic railing. The town sparkles down below me and it's magical looking. I can see the charm of a place such as this, which is contrary to my urban London roots.

The swish of the door sliding on its track catches my attention and

I turn to see Joslyn stepping out of the master bedroom. She's got on a pair of pajamas that look like they would be considered comfy but I find them sexy as fuck. A long sleeved, soft-looking pink cotton top and a pair of brown pants that are cinched at her ankles with large pink polka dots all over them. Her hair is wrapped up in a towel and her face is freshly scrubbed.

"It's beautiful at night, isn't it?" she asks as she comes to stand beside me at the railing. She mimics me by putting her forearms on the rails.

"Sure is," I tell her.

"Where's Jayce?" she asks conversationally.

"Down there somewhere," I say with a nod of my head down at the cozy evening lights of the small town. Jayce asked if I minded if he went down for a few beers and I didn't at all. He was off duty and as long as he was alert and ready to be primary watch on Joslyn tomorrow, I was cool with it.

Not that I planned to stay in the suite with Joslyn tonight for any length of time. I planned on hanging out in my room since we were securely locked inside the suite.

In reality, though, I didn't want the temptation of being in a place alone with her. At the apartment, her mom was always there. Granted, after a certain hour, she retired to her room but still... she was just yards away from us.

Here... alone with Joslyn... just might be too much temptation for me. I'm smart enough to have figured out that Joslyn is as attracted to me as I am her. We've flirted enough to know it's true. We've learned enough about each other to have the feelings of attraction compounded.

I don't know if I'm strong enough to resist her.

"I miss this weather," she murmurs and rubs briskly at her arms, despite the fact she's got wet hair under that towel and bare feet. "Fifty degrees at night in the middle of summer. Sleeping with the windows open and hunkered under a big fluffy comforter. That's the best sleep ever."

"Do me a favor and keep the sliding glass door closed," I tell her, not discounting those very slim odds someone would try to get at her that way. She's too precious to take that risk.

Yes, I've come to learn that about Joslyn.

She's precious to this world.

To me as well, but that can never go anywhere except the interior of my heart.

Joslyn laughs at my overprotectiveness, but it trails away naturally until there's nothing but silence for a moment. I think I could probably stand out here with her all night and just be quiet with her.

"I can't believe how much I've missed this place," she murmurs and I lean to one elbow to turn halfway toward her. She gives me a slight smile then looks back down to the town. "You know... if I never make it big, I do believe I could come back here and be very happy living as a normal, small town girl."

"What would you do?" I ask her curiously. We never talked about dreams she might have outside of singing.

"College for sure," she says as she tilts her head my way. "But what I'd study, no clue. I was never all that interested in school when I was in it. Always wanted to just be off singing."

"It's your passion," I remind her, something she knows deep down inside. "I don't think anything else will fulfill you. Damn good thing you're superb at it, because I think you're not going to have any problem becoming a star one day."

She blinks at me in surprise. "You really think so?"

"I do," I tell her confidently, at the same time hating it will inevitably take her away from Vegas and me.

"I wish I had that same confidence in myself that you have for me," she says wistfully as her gaze darts off to the side.

I wait for her to look at me again. When she does, I tell her, "I'll make sure to remind you several times a day until you know it's true."

I know the words are wrong the minute they leave my mouth. Her brow wrinkles and her eyes fill with emotion. "You really do believe in me, don't you?"

Walk away, McGrath, I tell myself. *Walk the fuck away.*

I take a step closer to her. "Yeah... I do."

Is it my imagination, or does she move closer to me?

I can't really figure it out, because my gaze is focused so intently on her face that everything else seems hazy.

"Do me a favor, Kynan," she whispers, and yes... I'll do anything she asks.

"What?"

"Kiss me." Her voice is feather light and yet her words almost knock me backward. My gut tightens, only to be swiftly followed by my groin.

Walk the fuck away.

"Not a good idea," I tell her, even as my hand touches her face. She leans into it, closes her eyes and purrs.

Fuck.

"Kiss me," she murmurs once again, opening her eyes and pinning those crystal blues on me. "Please."

And I'm done.

My fingers slide into her hair, wrapping around the base of her neck. I pull her gently toward me, leaning down at the same time.

Those lashes are so fucking long, I think, as her eyelids flutter and then close. Her hand comes up to wrap around my wrist, and she holds on to me tight.

Lips parting, breath hitching—that would be both of us—I am powerless to stop myself. My mouth touches hers, hesitates a moment, and then presses in. Joslyn opens for me just enough that I can give her a kiss that's not so deep as to say, "I want to fuck you" but is way more than a brush of possible desire.

But because there is a part of me that wants to pull her closer, crush her mouth under mine, and possess every single fucking inch of her, I let her go and back away. The kiss lasted but a few moments and yet they were the best moments of my life so far.

And that is why I have to fucking back away.

"We can't do this," I tell her, my voice gruff with lust and disappointment.

"Why?" she asks, the slight lilt of disgruntlement evident.

"Because you're my client, Joslyn. It's inappropriate. I'm here to protect you... not to... just... I can't."

The warmth in her eyes dies and her mouth flattens. "I don't think that's a good excuse."

"Maybe not," I tell her. "But I can't get involved with you while I'm protecting you."

"What if you weren't protecting me?" she asks.

"Were you not just participating in that kiss with me? What do you think?" My tone is sarcastic but teasing.

It makes her smile. It goes from amused to almost evil. She lifts her chin and says, "Then you're fired. Now kiss me."

Chuckling, I shake my head at her. "Not going to happen, Joslyn."

I turn for the door, intent on going to my room and taking a shower so I can jack off. Her hand shoots out and latches onto my forearm. It would never stop me but I give her the respect of my attention. I'd never walk away from her until she was cool with me walking away from her.

"What could possibly be wrong with you kissing me?" she asks, genuinely perplexed.

I step into her, backing her up against the railing. Bending down to put my face near hers, I tell her what she needs to know about getting involved with someone like me. "Joslyn... if I kiss you like I really want to kiss you, it's not going to end with anything less than me fucking your brains out."

It's crude and over the top, but she needs to know that the things I feel for her make me feel dangerous. She does not want me to unleash that on her, and I can't afford to ruin this fucking job when it happens.

"Oh," she breathes out in a long, fluttering rush of air.

"I can't get close to you like that," I tell her regretfully. "I have to stay removed a bit so I can stay objective when it comes to protecting you. It's just not good to mix business with..."

My words trail off, because I can't quite put my finger on why this is so dangerous.

"Pleasure?" Joslyn guesses.

I shake my head as it comes to me. "No. Enthrallment. You are the type of woman that would enthrall me to the point of confusion and distraction. I can't have that if I'm trying to protect you."

She only stares at me, measuring my words but giving me nothing in her expression to indicate if she understands what I mean. If she listened carefully—and reads between the lines—I just told her that I've never in my life felt for a woman the way I feel for her.

Finally, she nods and jerks her head toward the sliding door. I take the reprieve and leave the balcony. I give one last check of the main door, ensure it's locked and bolted, and then head into the adjoining room.

Straight to the bathroom where I strip, turn the shower on hot, and step inside to jerk myself off to the images of Joslyn in my mind.

Chapter 10

Joslyn

The band currently on stage is playing some classic country music, focusing on greats like George Strait and Willie Nelson. My dad loved country music and thus, so did I. I can even sing it halfway decently, but it's not what's true to my soul. That's always going to be pop rock à la the styles of Pink and Avril Lavigne with my own twist of Joslyn Meyers' funkiness to it.

I glance at my watch again. I'm waiting for my friend Carrie Foster to arrive. Jayce is loitering in the background, leaning up against a wooden fence that separates off an area of activities for younger kids. He watches me and the surroundings, doing his job. No clue where Kynan is. He went to the ribbon-cutting ceremony at the hospital with me this morning. Technically, Jayce was on duty but Kynan informed both of us that he'd be the one taking me to that. Jayce didn't question it but I did.

Did that mean he wanted to be with me during something that would undoubtedly be emotional? I'd like to think that was the reason, and I can't think of any other.

But I also don't want to read too much into it. Kynan stopped our kiss and made it clear he couldn't take this further.

I guess perhaps he merely went with me this morning as a friend to show support, and really... that meant the world. I shed a few tears and while he made no overt move to comfort me, I could see by the look on his face that he was sad that I was sad.

He dropped me off here at the concert venue where Jayce was waiting to take over. I assume he went back to the resort to rest up for my concert tonight.

"Jossy," I hear from my left and when I twist my body that way, I see Carrie waving at me as she weaves her way through the crowd listening to the music. I'd chosen a picnic table that sits off to the side of the concert area, which is set up in the Whitetail Parks baseball and soccer fields that border Whitetail Lake.

From here I can see several boaters out on the lake as well as jet skiers. The city beach is packed with people who are sunbathing while listening to the concert music. The summer tourist population swells to around fifteen thousand people who want to take advantage of the amazing climate for all kinds of outdoor activities. The lake here is one such popular place for people to spend their summer vacations.

Carrie reaches my table as I stand up, and we give each other a long, hard hug as we rock back and forth. She was my best friend in high school and, while we don't stay in touch nearly as much as we should, the bond is still there. I can thankfully feel it.

"God, you look great," she says as she holds my hands in hers and spreads my arms wide to take a look at me. "But then again, you always did. Had all the boys panting after you."

I roll my eyes and jerk my hands away from her. "Whatever. And besides, you're the one that looks amazing."

And she does. Her strawberry blonde hair is pulled back into her trademark ponytail. She's got on a hat to shield her fair complexion from the sun, lest her thousands of freckles turn into millions.

"Pfft," she says in response to my compliment, but that was always her way. She's one of the most humble people I know. She takes my hand and drags me down onto the picnic table bench. We sit facing each other and straddling the pine plank, grinning like fools.

"What do you want to do today?" I ask her. Because I'd planned to spend the entire day with Carrie. I'd actually invited several of the friends that had constituted our little group in high school, but everyone had plans except Carrie. I wasn't stupid though. I think they were personally avoiding me but I'm not sure why. I'm the same Joslyn Meyers I was when I left Cunningham Falls.

"Let's just sit here and talk a bit," Carrie says. "I've got so much to tell you, mostly about how Misty, Ella, and Christy are absolute bitches."

"I wondered why they didn't want to hang out," I say glumly. "Is it me?"

Carrie, never one to pull punches, nods at me. "They're jealous. That's all. Started when you won that talent show, then when your album dropped they still sort of hung on because everyone thought you'd be famous. When that didn't work out, they just turned catty but I wasn't about to tell you that. Not with dealing with your dad and everything. Now you're a big hit in Vegas, and they're more than jealous again. So I'm glad they didn't want to hang and it's just you and me today."

While my heart hurts a bit to know I could so easily lose friends—friends by the way who still text me as if we are still quite chummy—I'm fortified to know that Carrie never has wavered. Sure, we've not seen each other at all since I moved to Vegas, but she has been my one constant link back to my hometown. We try to talk at least a few times a month by phone and text far more than that.

After graduation, Carrie got a job working as a trail guide for an adventure company here and she loves it the way she loves Cunningham Falls. She'll never leave.

"Well, let's catch up," I suggest to her, more than willing to move on from the other girls. "Work going well?"

"I love it," she beams. "Hiking the back country in the summer and I'm going to start ski instructing in the winter months. I need to start making enough money so I can move out of my parents' place."

I give her a commiserating nod. "I totally get that. It's not all that easy to live with your parent."

"At least your mom is cool," she says, without really knowing about the conflicts we face on a daily basis as I struggle to understand her true role in my life. "My parents want me to stay home on Friday nights and play Scrabble with them."

The mention of the world Scrabble and my mind drifts off to Kynan.

And that kiss we shared last night.

A kiss that curled my toes, did the strangest of things to my body, and left me with insomnia most of the night. I was worried it would be weird in the morning, but he was just regular old Kynan with me. Ready to chat about anything or give me a cute grin when something amused him.

Such as how I started staring at his mouth while we were eating breakfast at Ed's Diner.

"Hello, Earth to Joslyn," Carrie says, snapping her fingers in front of my face. "Where did you go there?"

I blink at her and realize she must have been talking to me and I didn't hear a damn word of what she said. Further proof that I have Kynan rooted deeply in my mind and can't seem to shake him.

I look to my left and see Jayce in the same position. His head moves side to side as he surveys the crowd, in between bringing his gaze to me for a few moments. I scan the crowd around us, and don't see Kynan, but I didn't really expect to.

Giving my attention back to Carrie, I lean in closer to her. She immediately understands I'm about to unload something personal and potentially juicy, so she scoots closer to me and tilts her head expectantly.

"So... one of my bodyguards—"

"You have bodyguards?" she asks loudly and looks around. "Where are they?"

I grab her arm and tug on it to get her attention. "Don't look but one of them is standing over there against the fence."

Of course she looks. And then she ogles, which yeah... Jayce is kind of cute. But he's no Kynan.

"Are you hitting that?" she asks as she slowly turns her head back my way.

"No way," I exclaim.

"Can I hit it?" she asks.

I slap her on the arm and she grins at me.

"Anyway," I continue on. "One of my other bodyguards... Kynan."

"That's a great name," she says dreamily.

"He's British," I tell her and she sighs. Shaking my head, I move on with my story. "Anyway... we've gotten close, as in friendship. But there's this crazy attraction between us and you can feel it. It's hard to not give in to it, you know? And then last night... I asked him to kiss me, and he did, and Carrie... it was the most amazing thing I've ever experienced in my life."

Carrie stares at me when I finish talking.

She stares at me some more, like she expects more to the story.

When nothing is forthcoming, she slowly drawls, "Okay... tell me about the part where you had mind-blowing sex?"

My shoulders sag, as do my spirits. I shake my head. "He said we can't. That he's got a job to protect me and he can't get involved with me personally."

"So fire him," she suggests.

"One step ahead of you. I already tried it and it didn't work."

Carrie looks over to Jayce again, then back to me. "So what are you going to do? Just let it go? Because... you like this guy, right?"

"So much," I tell her softly. "He's all I think about."

"Does he feel the same way about you?" Her tone this time is hesitant and I can tell she wants to make sure I'm not being led on in any way.

I think about that for a moment, and realize I know something to be true. "I'm pretty sure he does. I felt it in that kiss, but more than that, it's in the way he talks to me. The interest he has in me. Not Joslyn the singing star, but in *me*. And he's opened up so much. He confides things he's never told anyone else."

Carrie leans forward with excitement. "Like what?"

"Like none of your business," I tell her primly. "That's for us to share alone."

"You have to do something," Carrie says adamantly. "I mean, this sounds pretty deep to me. You can't just not pursue him because his job will interfere."

"I don't want him to lose his job though." It's the only reason I didn't provoke him further last night. I don't want my selfishness to hurt him.

Carrie looks at something over my shoulder and her eyes go big with awe. I twist my neck, look behind me, and see Kynan walking our way.

"Is that him?" Carrie asks. "I mean... I figure it is. He's dressed the same way as the other dude over there, but damn, Jossy. You didn't tell me he was so freaking hot."

I ignore her and smile at Kynan as he approaches. He's incredibly hot but that's only one of the reasons I'm attracted to him.

The other is by what he has in his hand, which he offers to me. "Figured you could use one."

I take the venti caramel Frappuccino with whipped cream on top. He knows it's my favorite and he went out of his way to get me one.

"Thank you," I tell him and then sweep a hand toward Carrie. "This is my friend, Carrie Foster."

Kynan sticks his hand out to her and gives her a roguish smile that makes her giggle. I hold my laugh as they shake hands, enjoying seeing confident Carrie reduced to a school girl because Kynan is just that gorgeous.

Turning back to me, Kynan says, "I just touched base with Sheriff Hull. He seems to have security well in hand. Honestly, you'd be safe enough without me and Jayce at your back, but I'll be just off stage like I normally do in Vegas, okay?"

"Sounds like a plan," I tell him and then take a sip of the cool, creamy delight.

"You good?" he asks. "Need anything?"

I shake my head. "We're good. Just going to hang out awhile."

Kynan's brown eyes turn warm for a moment and they drop ever so briefly to my mouth. Is he thinking about our kiss? Would he do it again if I asked? Am I a complete slut if I ask?

"Okay then," he says and thumbs over his shoulder at Jayce. "He's got control of you. I'm going to walk around a bit. Call me when you want to go somewhere."

"I will," I murmur and then Carrie and I watch as Kynan melts back into the crowd.

She sighs first and I sigh right behind her.

"God, Jossy," she says. "You need to get all over that. That man is crazy about you."

My head whips back her way and my brow furrows. "What makes you say that?"

"Could you not see it on his face? Hear it in the way he talks to you? You walk on water for him and he'd cross fire for you."

I just blink at her.

"You don't see that?" she presses.

"I don't know," I admit miserably. "I feel something but I don't know what it is. I think it's only me sometimes, but then you say something like that and I think you might be right. There's something really amazing there between us."

"My advice is don't wait for it," she says with an emphatic nod. "Life is too short."

"Life is too short," I repeat.

"You should go for it," she pushes at me.

"Just go for it?" I echo back to her.

"Go for it," Carrie repeats. "What do you have to lose?"

A broken heart and a crushed spirit most likely.

But Kynan is probably worth risking those things.

Chapter 11

Kynan

I'd thought I'd seen Joslyn performing at her peak in Vegas. Her act is so entertaining you get lost in it. Her voice so beautiful time stands still. And when it's all over and done with, you want to push her back out there and tell her, "Do it again." Because I could watch her 24/7 on that stage and never get tired of it.

But now I realize that she wasn't even close to unleashing her potential. If any talent agent were watching her now, there'd be a mad stampede to get her signed.

I can only assume it's being back in her hometown and singing for her father's memory that is making the difference. The passion she's putting into her music tonight is transcendental. She doesn't have the fancy stage lighting, sparkling costumes, and high energy backup dancers behind her.

No, she's just in her jeans, a flowing taupe-colored blouse that bares one shoulder, and simple, flat sandals. She did her hair in loose braids hanging over each shoulder with wisps framing her face. Her makeup is simple and understated.

She's just Joslyn, yet a completely different one than I've ever seen before.

Tonight, she is simply magical, and years from now I might look back on this moment and say it was when I fell helplessly for her.

She's on her final song. It's one she sings in her Vegas act. The one on the stool with the lone spotlight on her. But tonight she just stands in front of the microphone, both hands clutching it hard and her lips moving fluidly as she sings about love and heartache and redemption.

I force myself to look around. The crowd is gently swaying to the tune, many singing along with her. Her best friend Carrie is in front, beaming up at her. Several times Joslyn has looked down at her during her performance and smiled back. It was nice to see Joslyn just have time with a friend today. She never gets to do enough fun things for herself. She's always working or rehearsing, and her evenings are spent talking to me, which can't be all that exciting.

Right?

I try not to think of that fucking kiss. The one that almost drove me to my knees and then later drove me to one of the hardest orgasms I'd ever had while I was in the shower jacking myself off. I felt simultaneously dirty to be doing it and accomplished. I've never been attracted to someone like this. I've never wanted to just lose myself in another person before, and I feel sometimes I could gladly give up my existence to just immerse myself in hers.

It's both exciting and terrifying at the same time, but ultimately it's moot. She's a client, not a romantic interest.

Joslyn's song comes to an end and before the last notes of the backup band's music fade away, she pulls the mic closer to her mouth and waves to the crowd. "Thank you, Cunningham Falls, for all your support to raise money for cancer research today. I've missed this place so much, and it's been great to be back. I love you."

The crowd cheers and people clap while calling out for an encore. Lighters flare to life and smartphones are held up to shine light. It's not something she can indulge in Vegas. When the show is over, it's over.

But here she's the final act of the night.

There are no rules.

She looks out over the crowd, her bottom lip quivering ever so slightly with emotion. She turns her head and looks at me. I smile and nod to her, telling her she needs to give them more.

She grins back at me and I'm simply dazzled. We stare at each other a moment before Joslyn turns to walk back to the band. The lead guitarist leans in toward her, she says something to him, and he turns to relay the message to the other musicians.

Joslyn takes the mic again, the music strikes up, and she gives the crowd more.

* * * *

"Are you sure you don't want to stay out tonight?" I ask Joslyn as we ride back to the resort in the rented SUV. Jayce stayed back for the evening carnival and because I think he hooked up with someone last night and intended to do the same again tonight.

Fine by me. He's off duty and while absolutely nothing would ever happen, I like having Joslyn to myself.

"No," she says quietly as she leans back in the passenger seat. "I'm done for the night."

She sounds tired, which she often is after a performance. Still, I thought she'd want to hang with Carrie for a bit. Instead, after she finished her last double encore song, she came off the stage and just rested a hand lightly on my forearm. "I'm going to go say goodbye to Carrie, then I'll be ready to call it a night."

Her voice was huskier than normal but she sang way longer than she normally does. Her eyes looked fatigued but her body still seemed to have bounce in her step.

It worries me, so I ask her one more time. "You sure? Last night in Cunningham Falls. I could take you back down to the beach. They're serving huckleberry ice cream."

Her head rolls to the left and she gives me a smile that I can read nothing into. "I'm sure."

With a sigh, I push the gas pedal down to start the climb up Whitetail Mountain and the ski resort at the top.

Joslyn is silent for the ride and it's throwing me off a bit because she's such a chatterbox normally. I know she's riding a bit of an adrenaline high because I'm betting that was the most fun she's ever had performing.

Is she upset about me pulling out of the kiss last night? Does she know it has nothing to do with her and everything to do with my job? That I'd cut off my right nut if Jerico would tell me it would be fine to guard her and have her at the same time?

More silence as I park. We cross the parking lot to the lobby and ascend to the room in the elevator. I watch her carefully and she doesn't seem upset. She catches me watching her and gives me back a fond smile.

And that's confusing.

Maybe she's moved on. Maybe when I told her that we couldn't be together, she took me at face value and she's already let it go.

Let me go.

"Joslyn," I say as we reach the room, turning to block the door. "Are you okay?"

She blinks at me in surprise, noting the worry in my voice. "Of course I am. Why do you ask?"

"I just thought you'd want to stay out, this being your last night in Cunningham Falls, and you've been awful quiet since we left the venue."

Again, she smiles and shakes her head. "That performance was just... so amazing, I kind of just want to revel in that. I don't want to lose this feeling."

I'm immediately relieved and I feel my body loosen. A sense of joy sweeps through me that she got as much out of that performance as I did. That it was just as magical to her as it was to me.

Joslyn tilts her head quizzically as she stares at me. "You felt it too, didn't you?"

"The magic?" I ask her, then clarify. "Your magic."

"There's only been one other time I can think of that I was so in tune with my feelings," she murmurs, her eyes taking on a dreamy quality.

And it hits me like a nuclear warhead slamming into my chest.

I know exactly what she's talking about when she says she's only felt this amazing, mystical, magical quality once before.

It was our kiss last night.

"Joslyn," I whisper, my hands clenching into fists so I don't grab her to me.

"Did you feel it too?" she asks me in a low voice. "Last night?"

"Down to the marrow of my fucking bones," I growl at her. "You know that, right? That I felt as much of it as you did and it was the hardest fucking thing to pull away from you."

Her expression turns sad and she nods. "Yeah... I know."

I merely stare at her. I'm barking mad over her and I don't know what to do. I want to beg her to disregard all of my concerns over us being together. I want her to tell me it's stupid and that we can make it work.

Or not quite what I want but at least more appropriate, I want her to be the adult and tell me that I'm doing the right thing by leaving her alone. It would ease my conscience for sure.

Instead, her gaze lowers and she turns to the door while pulling the card key from her purse. I feel like I've killed her good mood because I know mine sure as hell is gone.

The door unlocks and I feel I'm moments away from losing her. I can't explain this irrational feeling but I know it to be true.

There's no explaining my actions other than I let my heart have control and it tells my brain to shut the fuck up. I grab her arm and turn her around toward me. I get a brief moment to see her eyes flare with surprise before I have my hands on her face and my mouth on hers.

She moans in surprise and pleasure, the sound all at once driving away any last bit of rationality I had. Coming off a night listening to the best that Joslyn has to offer to the world, knowing that it was a transcendental experience as was the kiss I gave her, I choose to no longer listen to my conscience and instead take what deep in my heart I know to be all mine.

I press her slight frame into the door and find her tongue with mine. She moans again, but it's drowned out by my groan of relief at having her mouth. The shared lust between us is palpable and it causes my cock to go hard as a rock. One more moan from her when her hips lift to meet mine and she feels the thick ridge of my shaft.

I about lose my shit when she drops a hand down and cups me so softly, I can barely feel her. But my balls tingle and I pray to fucking God I don't come just from that slight touch.

Even with that embarrassment at risk, I dare not remove my lips from hers. I deepen the kiss as I drop my hand. It goes to the apex of her legs. To her secret spot and she parts for me. I press my palm to her, feel the warmth through her jeans, and my mouth waters wondering just how magical she'll taste.

Joslyn bucks from the contact and I use the opportunity to slip the keycard from her hand. I somehow find the slot, get the door open, and push her inside. I do all of this while kissing the everloving fuck out of her, and I don't stop because to do so would be akin to dying.

I bend, easily lift her to my body, and almost shout into her mouth with joy when she wraps her legs tightly around me.

She presses her hands to my cheeks and pulls away from the kiss just enough that she can murmur into my mouth. "You better not stop, Kynan," she warns me.

It's adorable.

I answer her by walking into the master bedroom and tossing her down on the bed. I kick the door closed and reach back to lock it. Then I pull my shirt slowly over my head and let it drop to the floor.

She watches me with eyes of dark denim, or maybe it's her pupils that have shadowed her look. I smile at her. "I'm not stopping. Ever."

Joslyn raises a hand, beckoning me to the bed.

Not ever stopping.

Chapter 12

Joslyn

It's happening.

It. Is. Happening.

My mouth goes dry as Kynan slowly peels his black Jameson shirt over his head. His abs contract, forming a washboard, and I get mesmerized by a dragon tattoo rippling up his ribs and across part of his chest.

He's simply too beautiful for words, and one day I need to sit down and write a song about that type of beauty. The kind that makes you mindless with need, to where you think you might die if you have to wait another single moment for it to touch you.

Kynan discards the shirt and walks to the bed. I'm sitting near the edge where he dropped me but it's apparently not what he wants. He merely lifts me up easily under my armpits, puts a knee to the bed, and then pushes me down with his big body coming on top of me.

He kisses me again, ever so slowly, and I can tell he's not in a rush.

This.

Our first time together.

It's further proven when his hands oh so slowly wander over my body but going no further than feathering across the top of my clothing. The faintest touch to my breast or a light drag of his knuckles between my legs. I am drowning in need and I feel like I want to cry.

"Please," I moan as his lips move from my mouth to the side of my neck.

"What do you want, Jos?" he asks in a husky voice.

"You," I pant as he bites the skin where my neck meets my shoulder.

Kynan lifts his head and smiles down at me. "I'll give you anything you want."

"I want you to make love to me," I beg him, because he's already driven me crazy with his soft, slow touches.

"I will," he murmurs. "First with my mouth, then with my cock."

A shudder rips up my spine and my eyes flutter closed at the thought of it. I've never... done that. I've had sex, and it wasn't good, but never had a man's mouth...

I go instantly wet and start to squirm. Kynan takes pity on me and helps me out of my clothing, all the while stealing kisses in between. When my breasts are bared to him, he sucks hard on one of my nipples and an ache starts deep in my core.

After he gets me naked, Kynan pushes off the bed and quickly divests himself of his clothing. His underwear are the last to come off and I can't help but stare at the most magnificent part of his body sticking up tall, thick, and straight with desire for me.

I ogle him and want badly to take him in my hand... my mouth. Any way I can touch him there to give him pleasure.

I even start to reach out to him, but he gives me a chastising shake of his head. My brains practically scramble from the heat he causes when he drops to the floor on his knees and pulls me roughly by the legs to the edge of the mattress. He spreads me wide and I flush with embarrassment as he stares at my most private parts, and it's with reverence as well as hunger.

Then he puts his mouth on me and it's a pleasure that I didn't know existed. No matter how many times I've touched myself in the very exact spot he has his tongue, I could never be prepared for this onslaught of feelings. The deep intimacy that we're sharing right now causes tears to well in my eyes, and when Kynan groans in approval—no, gratitude—over what he's tasting, I know I'll never feel for another man the way I feel for him.

He licks at me gently, and then sucks. He presses fingers into me and lashes his tongue harder. My head spins and my core aches, and then I'm exploding so hard that my hips shoot off the mattress. Kynan presses me back down, moving his face so lewdly between my legs that another harsh ripple of pleasure pulls me apart. I cry his name out and he gives another satisfied grunt as he continues to kiss between my legs.

I feel coolness there, so I open my eyes. I see the ceiling then I lift my head to find Kynan pulling a condom out of his wallet. He's practiced and efficient with getting it out and rolling it on.

He's walking toward me, his big hand wrapped around his shaft, and I scramble backward toward the headboard. Kynan grins as he places a knee to the bed before climbing his way up me. The last thing I see before spreading my legs and accepting his mouth on mine is his warm brown eyes watching me like I'm the most cherished thing in the world.

He kisses me and I taste myself on his tongue. Kynan shifts and I feel him pressing against me. Shifting again, then into me. I stretch, focusing on the kiss instead of the slight bite of pain because he's a bit bigger than what I experienced before.

He pulls his hips back, never taking his lips from mine. A slight thrust and he's a bit deeper. He does this over and over again, working himself into me as if we have all the time in the world. My body was sated for several moments from my orgasm, but when he manages to press his entire length into me, I feel the churn of lust starting to build again.

Kynan lifts his head and looks down at me. "You okay?"

"Never better," I whisper with a smile.

He gives me one back and it's so beautiful. I expect him to kiss me again, but he doesn't. He just moves his face a little closer to mine and stares right into my eyes. I feel him withdraw, hate losing the fullness of our connection, but before I can complain he's thrusting back in again.

"Oh," I grunt as he fills me up so deeply my eyes roll in the back of my head.

"You are the best thing I've ever felt in my life, Joslyn," he tells me in a voice so earnest while he never lets his eyes leave my face, that I know he's telling me the truth. His forehead drops until it touches mine and he whispers, "So fucking good."

Kynan moves inside of me. Our hands end up clasped so tightly together my fingers ache. His thrusts become deeper, delivered with a powerful punch. Every one feels better and better.

Another orgasm starts to brew. I concentrate on the feel of him and how his pelvis manages to rub at my most sensitive spot with each drive of himself into me.

He makes love to me so beautifully that I know my life won't be the same after.

We move together, undulating and writhing. He whispers to me how beautiful I am, and even tells me he's never tasted anything better. I flush with heat and then he drives up into me hard. I start to break apart, and my hands move to clutch frantically to his shoulders. I press my legs tight to his hips and I share with him what is happening.

"I'm coming again." I murmur my surprise as well as my relief. I need this. My body needed to be released as he built me up.

"Yes," he says like he's delivering up a prayer. He starts to move faster, punching in harder. My orgasm rumbles on and on, and I wonder if it will ever stop. Kynan's chest heaves and his eyes squeeze shut for just a brief moment.

He then goes unbelievably still within me and his eyes fly open. They latch onto mine and he groans, "I'm coming, Jos."

His jaw locks tight and his face looks almost pained, but his words are beautiful as he grits them out. "Coming. So. Fucking. Hard."

Kynan shudders in my arms and I try to gather him to me. I wrap my legs all the way around his back and lock him in with my ankles. I squeeze and contract my interior muscles and I know he feels it because he groans and shudders even harder. I close my eyes and feel this man orgasming inside of me and I've never felt closer to another human being in my life.

Huffing out a breath, Kynan lets his body weight sag onto me and then rolls slightly to his side. His arms gather me close and he pulls me into his chest. I place my ear there and love the music of his galloping heart. I think I'll write a song about it and memorialize the beat of post orgasmic relief.

"You're amazing, Jos," Kynan murmurs. The words are simple but the tone and meaning I hear within them shock me.

I pull my head back, wanting to see his face. He regards me with clear eyes, in no way befuddled with the haze of amazing sex. He nods, as if he understands that I'm questioning this. He puts his face closer to me, and repeats, "More amazing than anything I've ever felt in my life."

And the tears come. He doesn't get alarmed because I smile through them. As he takes a thumb and wipes one away, I touch his face with my fingertips. I want to tell him I love him, but how can I when this is all so new? He'd think me young and impetuously silly.

So instead I just tell him, "I'm so happy right now. I think this is the best night of my entire life."

"I'm glad," he murmurs, putting his palm to the back of my head as a means to hold me close.

We lie in silence for a bit before Kynan tells me, "I can't stay with you all night. I don't want Jayce to know."

I push away from him slightly so I can see his face. "That would be bad," I agree.

"I'm going to have to resign when we get back. I'll go see Jerico tomorrow after we land."

"Oh, God," I exclaim as guilt floods my body. "No. I don't want you to lose your job."

"It's fine," he reassures me.

His voice is calm and sure, but I feel wretched. "There has to be some way—"

"Joslyn, I can't do my job effectively. I can't treat you like just some client I have to protect. It's best I resign."

"I feel awful," I tell him.

"Don't," he says, placing fingers over my lips. "What you and I have here is more important than any job. I'll land something else quick, so don't worry, okay?"

I just stare at him.

"Okay?" he repeats.

Finally, I have to nod and he removes his hand from my mouth. He replaces it with his mouth and the kiss isn't sweet at all. It's a claiming kiss that lets me know that I belong to him, and past that, nothing else really matters.

Chapter 13

Kynan

I enter the lobby of the Jameson Group offices. We still haven't hired a receptionist and I doubt we will until we finish up the casino project and start building up our clientele. Until such time, no sense in paying someone to sit out here just to greet the employees coming in.

Making my way to Jerico's office, I wonder how Joslyn is faring. From the airport, I dropped her and Jayce off at her apartment and then headed straight here. She's going to be telling her mom about us and I'm going to be resigning. We decided to just get it done with so people can get over the shock, and then hopefully support us.

I merely hope to come away with my friendship with Jerico intact. I'm struggling with the guilt of letting him down and doing exactly what he told me not to do.

The heart, however, wants what it wants, and I've realized it's the most powerful organ in our body. There's apparently no arguing or reasoning with it.

Jerico's office isn't much to write home about. I expect he'll fill it with nice furniture like that in the lobby to give the impression of an incredibly successful company. It just hasn't been high on his list, and as of now, he merely has a desk set up in the center of the room. Granted, it's a nice desk—dark cherry, heavy and masculine. He's also got a huge leather chair behind it that holds his big frame easily.

He's sitting in it when I tap on the already open door, reading something on his laptop. Glancing up, he gives me a smile and jerks his head for me to enter.

"How'd everything go in Cunningham Falls?" he asks as I walk toward his desk. There are no chairs for me to sit in.

"Smooth sailing," I tell him as I assume a military stance in front of him. What I'd really like to do is act all casual and just sort of tuck my hands in the pockets of my utility cargos, but that seems too casual. I know one thing... I will miss this uniform, as it's pretty badass.

"Great," he says and then looks back to his laptop. "You should get home and get some rest before you take over the evening shift."

"Yeah," I drawl hesitantly and that causes his head to snap up. "About that. There's a problem with me guarding Joslyn."

Jerico's eyebrows draw inward but his voice is merely inquisitive. "What problem?"

"We slept together last night," I tell him bluntly. Might as well get to the real issue—that would be the one he'd fire me for. "I'm here to resign or you can fire me, but I get that I can't stay on because of that breach of ethical duty."

Jerico's jaw locks tight and he curses at me through gritted teeth. "Fuck, Kynan. I told you to stay away from her."

"Kind of hard, mate, when I'm guarding her twelve hours a day," I reply smoothly and he doesn't appreciate my flippancy.

"You know what I mean," he grows. "I told you not to fall for her."

"Also easier said than done when I'm spending so much time with her."

"Got an answer for everything, don't you?" His tone has gone cool and detached, and I'm afraid the friendship may have just bitten the dust.

I don't answer right away, trying to formulate my thoughts so he understands me. "Listen... I know what I did was wrong. I also know that I'm compromised. I'm too biased and that would affect my ability to protect her. I also know this puts you in a totally shitty situation with her mother. So I'm here to offer my sincere apology, mate, as well as my resignation. I truly hope this doesn't affect our friendship."

Jerico squeezes his eyes shut and pinches the bridge of his nose while muttering, "Jesus fucking Christ, Kynan."

"I'm sorry," I repeat. "I know this leaves you in a bad position with Madeline, but I know you can easily assign someone to take my place."

Jerico opens his eyes, glares at me, and then gives a dismissive wave.

"I can handle Madeline. What I can't handle is your resignation. You're my number two and my number three doesn't have nearly the qualifications or inherent abilities to move upward."

"What are you saying?" I ask him cautiously.

"I'm saying I'm not accepting your resignation," he snaps. "You can move over to help me manage the casino projects and I'll reassign someone to cover your shift tonight with Joslyn."

This was more than I had ever expected. I know Jerico says he can handle Madeline but the truth is, she's more than likely to fire us for this breach of trust. I'm sure she's going to think I took advantage of Joslyn, which might partly be true because, let's face it... I didn't have to kiss her last night.

I certainly could have chosen not to fuck her.

Wait... strike that.

Not all the military forces in the world could have stopped me from doing that last night, nor could they stop me today. She's mine and that's all there is to it.

"Is this thing serious with her?" Jerico asks, and that catches me off guard. I wasn't prepared to discuss the personal feelings involved.

But this is also Jerico Jameson. I'm incredibly tight with the bloke and we've been through some intense, dangerous stuff together that tends to bond you tighter than any regular friendship could. Maybe I misjudged his interest in my happiness outside of the workplace.

I decide to go with straight-up honesty, even it if makes me look like a pussy in his eyes. Up until now, both of us were happy playing the field with no intention of ever settling down.

"I don't know what this is," I tell him, lifting my chin just a bit in defiance of any laughter he might decide to throw my way. I'm prepared to punch him if he does anything to diminish it. "But I've never felt this before and I don't want to give it up."

He surprises me. Instead of ridicule or an incredible lewd joke, his eyes soften and the corners of his mouth tip up. "Then I'm happy for you. Truly."

I'd hug the guy if that totally wouldn't cause him to call me a pussy, but I smile back. "Thanks, mate."

"This is more than just lust, right?" he asks for clarification.

"It was something big before we were even together last night," I explain and my ears flush with heat. I feel proprietary over Joslyn and sharing our intimate details, even with someone I'm close to like Jerico. I don't want to cheapen anything about her.

Jerico sighs and leans back in his chair. "When she makes it big and leaves Vegas, you going with her?"

"I have no clue. I don't think that's happening any time soon. She still has a few months left on her Vegas contract, and when that's done, if she leaves I'll just have to figure things out then."

He regards me a moment and then mutters, "I should just fire you now because you'll probably be chasing her in a few months."

He's probably not wrong about that.

Jerico nods toward the door. "Go home and get some rest. I'll start you on the casino project tomorrow and I've got to call Madeline."

"Sure thing," I say and start to turn away. But then I look back at him. "Thanks, Jerico. Means the world you understanding."

"Can't say as I understand it," he drawls with a smirk. "But I believe and trust in your feelings. It's all good."

I nod my thanks and head out the door.

When I reach my car, I grab my phone and check my texts. I was hoping Joslyn would have been done talking to her mom and sent me some type of update. I see nothing but there is a missed call from Rachel Hart.

In moments, I have the voice mail rolling on speaker phone. *Hey, dude. Mate. Whatever the hell you Brits say. Just rolled into Vegas for a few weeks and thought I'd look you up. I'm going to do some climbing over at Red Rock Canyon and wanted to see if you were interested. Call me.*

I smile as I delete the voice mail.

I'll call her back later, as Rachel will be in town awhile and I'll definitely have to hook up with her for a climb.

Rachel is one of those chicks who can just "be one of the guys." Don't get me wrong... she's smokin' hot, but I've not gone there and don't intend to. We met less than a year ago in Venezuela. I was taking a month off for a long holiday before going to work at my father's car dealership, and because I'm an adrenaline junkie, I decided to do some base jumping off Angel Falls.

I jumped in a wingsuit and apparently Rachel had been up there and watched me. She came down via parachute, but immediately sought me out and asked me how to do it. She shared the same love of speed and danger as I did.

We've kept in touch since then with promises if we were ever in the same corner of the world again, we'd make plans to get our fix together.

I wonder if Joslyn would jump out of a plane with me. My guess is probably not, but that makes me adore her all the more. I make a mental note to call Rachel later to make plans, and instead dial Joslyn's number. I'm anxious to hear how things are going with her mother.

I'm only anxious because Joslyn's nervous about it. I could give a fuck what Madeline thinks of me personally and I'm pretty sure she's not going to be happy about this because she doesn't want Joslyn's focus anywhere but her career. I can handle any animosity she might throw my way but I'll be bloody pissed if she takes it out on her daughter.

Joslyn doesn't answer and I get her voice mail. I don't bother leaving a message but instead shoot a quick text to her. *All went fine with Jerico. He wouldn't let me resign and I didn't get fired. Call me after you talk to your mom.*

I debate for a moment whether or not to end it on an endearment. This is new territory for me and I don't want to fail her expectations, but I have no clue what they may be.

To be safe though, I say what's in my heart. *Can't wait to see you tonight.*

We've made plans to have an early dinner before she has to leave for her show. We also made tentative plans for her to come to my place after her show. I plan on being there to watch it, and I plan on driving her right back to my place whether Madeline likes it or not. Joslyn and I talked about this and she's ready to live her life as an adult and out from under her mother's constant thumb.

She can't stay all night, though. I told her that we needed to be a little mindful of her mother's feelings and be a little respectful of that. Still, I'm assuming gradually and over time, Joslyn will just naturally end up at my place permanently, and then it will become "our" place.

Yeah... that has a nice ring to it.

Chapter 14

Joslyn

I hate that I'm nervous as I put the key into the apartment door. Jayce takes up a post in the hallway. He never hangs out in the apartment the way Kynan did, but then again, I never invited him to. There's something about him that doesn't inspire the warm and fuzzies.

"Joslyn," my mother exclaims, and she's there to greet me as I'm closing the door. She wraps me in a warm hug, which is a rarity these days, and it surprises me so much, it takes me a moment to reciprocate.

My mom, dad, and I were always an openly affectionate family. From as early as I can remember, my mom always had a place for me on her lap. Throughout the years, I never questioned her love or loyalty to me. The affection between us was easy and natural, and yet it started to disappear when I entered show business.

Or rather, when she became my business manager. I came to understand why she changed as I rationalized it was too hard for her to be tough with me on the business side of things and loving to me on the mom side of things.

She had to pick a side, and she chose being a business manager as her primary role. This was okay with me because I couldn't do any of this without her, and as I got older, I was secure enough to know she loved me without the physical reassurance of hugs.

It feels nice hugging her now, and I squeeze her back extra tight.

"I missed you," I tell her, because I did. We've been together for so long and rarely are apart.

She pulls back from the hug but keeps her hands on my shoulders. She tries to contain it but fails, and the most enthusiastic smile I've ever seen graces her face. "You'll never guess what?"

"What?" I ask with a laugh.

"Ian's here in Vegas," she proclaims like a giddy schoolgirl. "He has the contract to represent you, and he says he already has an offer for you that is so big, we're not going to believe it."

"Oh," I say softly, not expecting that at all.

"Oh?" she teases me as her hands drop from my shoulders. She clasps them in front of her chest and practically hops in place with excitement. "Is that all you have to say? Come on, Joslyn... this is it. Your big break. And while I have no idea what kind of offer he's been given for you, he told me that he was taking us both out to the most expensive restaurant in Vegas for a celebratory meal tonight. We have to meet him at 6PM so you need to make sure you're ready to go at 5:30. He's going to send a car for us."

My head is spinning with all of this, but the only thing that can come out of my mouth is, "But I have plans tonight."

The expression on my mom's face changes into one of blank confusion. "Plans? What plans could be more important, and for that matter, why aren't you excited about this?"

"I'm just shocked," I tell her sincerely. "As soon as it sinks in, I'm sure I'll be jumping up and down with you. But I really can't do dinner tonight."

Her face morphs again and now she's pissed. "What could possibly be more important?"

And now it's time to tell her my big news, except now I've been set up to completely fail. I expected her to be mad and upset over my relationship with Kynan but by telling her I have plans tonight, I've set him up as being more important to me than my career or her, and that's not good at all.

"Mom," I say as I reach forward to take her hands. They're ice cold and I give them a squeeze. "I've got something to tell you."

"Oh my God," she moans as she pulls her hands away and looks at me in horror. "You're pregnant?"

"What? No. That's ridiculous."

She doesn't look relieved by my adamant denial. There's no way I can sugar coat this either, so I go all in.

"I'm seeing Kynan McGrath," I tell her with my spine straight and my chin lifted proudly. "We're in a relationship. A serious one and well... that's who I have plans with tonight. They had already been made first, you see, so I can't cancel. If Ian had called ahead of time or checked—"

"Joslyn Rae Meyers," she hisses through her teeth. "This is not funny at all."

I pull myself up and throw my shoulders back, resolved to defend myself and my feelings for Kynan. "I am not saying it to be funny. I think I'm falling in love with him. In fact, I've never felt this way before and—"

"Of course you've never felt this way before," she snaps. "You're nineteen. You know nothing of the world and men and love. Trust me, something better than him will come along one day."

"No, it won't," I say softly but with determination enunciating every syllable. "I know you must think me young and foolish, but he is the one for me and nothing you say will change it."

My mom waves her hand at me dismissively and gives me her back, walking toward the kitchen. "Don't be silly, Joslyn. I'm sure you were an easy target for him. I have to say though, I'm incredibly disappointed in this company. Assigning someone like that to your protection. I'm sure he took advantage of you and your vulnerability."

I follow her into the kitchen, my blood boiling so hot I feel I could detonate as she talks.

She picks up her phone and says, "I'm going to call them right now and terminate our services. We can find someone else tomorrow."

"Mom," I snap at her but she ignores me.

Instead, she flips through her contacts and keeps talking. "Yes, I'm quite sure he took advantage of you."

"He did not," I yell at her and snatch the phone from her hands. My mom blanches and blinks at me in surprise as her mouth forms into a tiny "O." "I made the first move. I asked him to kiss me, but before that, we had become really good friends. This isn't some passing fancy for me. It's real."

She stands still, rooted to the spot. The paleness of her complexion recedes and starts turning red over my audacity. I press my advantage while I can. "You don't have to worry about having him fired. He's resigning."

And now, she seems to not have anything to say. My mom merely stands there and just stares at me as if she has no clue who I am. Has no idea what I just said.

I have nothing further to say, though, as I've said the most important part. That Kynan is now an important part of my life, and that he's going to have priority with many things.

Finally, she speaks and it's with a voice so quiet, I can barely hear her. "I don't like this, Joslyn. You have a career that is getting ready to skyrocket. Whatever Ian has for us, I think it's bigger than you ever dared dream. You have to be ready to make a big move and if you're involved with someone, it will tie you down. It will diminish your dreams."

"No, it won't." I immediately put forth my denial.

"Yes, it will," she says sadly. "It will distract you. Trust me, I know. I remember what young love was like. Also trust this... this is not the best thing for you right now."

I inhale a deep breath, hold it a moment, and ask for peace to fill me. After I exhale, I tell her, "You can't dictate what my heart feels. You can't have sole discretion to decide what's best for me. Now, I can't expect you to understand what's inside me because even I can't put it quite into intelligible words, but I do expect you—as my mother—to respect my feelings. If you can't do that, Mom, we are going to have issues going forward."

I did it. For the first time in my singing career, I've just stood up to my business manager—or mom—however you choose to look at it. I staked my position and I'm not budging.

As she considers what I said, she must see something in my bearing that leads her to believe what I'm saying. That makes her understand that I can't be pushed right now, and I'm not going to relent where Kynan is concerned. It may be new to me, but that makes it all the more precious and I must protect it.

"Okay," she says with a slow nod of her head and a forced smile. "Fine. Date Kynan. I hope it brings you great joy. But please, please... do me the favor of not standing Ian up tonight. This is too important to blow off and if you and Kynan really care for each other, you'll have thousands of other opportunities to go out to dinner with him. If you don't see Ian tonight, you may never have another chance again."

My body sags with relief because I caught the most important words she could have given me.

Fine. Date Kynan.

I have her blessing on that and she respects that he's important to me.

That makes me feel generous and also because I know she's right, I can't miss what could be the meeting of a lifetime in regard to my career, I give her back a little peace of mind. "Of course I'll come to dinner tonight. I can't pass up this opportunity and Mom... I am excited about this. Thank you for working so hard to make it happen."

This mollifies her a tiny bit. I get a half smile but she still manages a disapproving tone in her voice. "Well, thank you for recognizing my hard work. I really have put my heart and soul into securing this contract with Ian. Just promise me you won't let anything distract you from your rise upward. You are moving up and I don't want that to get derailed by some—"

"I promise," I interject, before she can denigrate what I have with Kynan.

"Okay, then," she says stiffly. "I'm just going to run out on a quick errand. Make sure you're ready to go when I return at 5:30PM. And wear that black dress... the one with the capped sleeves."

"Sure," I say genially, accepting that she still needs to have some control.

When she leaves, I pull my phone out of my purse. The minute I turn it on, I see Kynan's text and I can't contain the yip of excitement that pops out of my mouth.

I don't bother responding but dial him instead.

He answers almost immediately. "How did it go?"

Rather than give him the info he requested, I can't help but share my excitement about his job. "You didn't have to resign. I'm so relieved. I was feeling just awful about it."

"It's cool, love," he says and I get all tingly over him calling me "love." It's so classically British but it's the tone that makes it extra special. "Now tell me how it went on your end."

"Mom wasn't as accepting but I got her on board with it," I tell him. "But I can't see you tonight for dinner like we'd planned."

"Why?" he asks curiously but in no way put out. "What's up?"

I'm relieved he can roll with changes in plans, but then again, Kynan is so laid back, I figured he would. "Apparently Ian is here in Las Vegas and wants to meet for dinner. He has a contract for representation for me to sign, and apparently I've had some type of big offer already he wants to tell me about."

"That's awesome, Joslyn," Kynan exclaims with enthusiasm. "I'm proud of you."

"Thanks," I say with a smile on my face but also a sadness in my heart. I have the sinking feeling that good things are coming my way but they may take other good things away from me. "Will you still come to my show tonight?"

"Wild horses couldn't keep me away," he tells me.

"And um... can we still go to your place after?" I ask hesitantly, my face heating up. I want to feel him again. On me, inside of me, all over me, but it's embarrassing to me to ask.

Kynan chuckles darkly and lowers his voice. My skin prickles when he says, "You bet your arse you're coming over. You have no idea the things I have planned for you."

For a brief moment, I consider saying to hell with my career and just taking an Uber to wherever Kynan is right now so I can demand he do the things he just promised.

But I can't, and I'm laughing when I tell him I can't wait to see him later.

Chapter 15

Kynan

Cash Sorles stands outside of Joslyn's dressing room as I walk down the hall. I wasn't sure who Jerico would replace me with, but he's a good choice. He doesn't have any military background but sure as hell knows a lot about guns and hand-to-hand combat. I need to make time to take him out for a beer and find out his back story. I know it's got to be interesting.

He sees me coming and lifts his chin. "What's up?"

"Not much," I tell him. Pointing at the door, I ask, "She in there by herself?"

Cash nods and doesn't seem surprised to see me here. That tells me he knows I'm involved with her and that's why he is now on guard duty. He also doesn't seem to be amused by it, which is good as I'd hate to have to impart some manners to him if he were to think it funny.

I give a two-knuckle rap against the door and wait for Joslyn to call me in. I step over the threshold, and then I barely get the door closed before she's flying across the tiny room to launch herself into my arms. It's the first time we've seen each other since I dropped her off today from the airport but even that is enough time for doubts to arise in such a new relationship, especially since we both have had some major things happening in the hours since.

I'm immediately relieved to see that she's as happy to see me as I am her, and I'm also incredibly aroused as her mouth seals onto mine for a deep, hot kiss. My hands palm her ass and squeeze, and I try to think if we have time to fool around before someone would barge in on us.

That's like a cold bucket of water dropped on me as I know that her mom and Michel are probably lurking around somewhere.

I no sooner let her slide down my body, ending the kiss with a tiny peck to her forehead, than the door is pushing open behind me. I move both Joslyn and me out of the way, and Michel sashays in.

I have to say, I thought it really weird that Joslyn was friends with a gay man that was twelve years her senior, but after spending the first five minutes in their presence together, I got it. They're a lot alike in their core personalities. Both incredibly caring, to the point they defer to others' happiness, and they both share the same sense of humor. I never questioned the age difference since.

"Hey, girlfriend and boyfriend," he chirps as he carries his huge makeup case over to the vanity. He doesn't pay us any mind, and he starts unloading his wares.

Leaning toward Joslyn, I whisper in her ear. "Did you tell Michel about us?"

"Yes," she whispers back. "And frankly, I'm surprised he's not making a big deal about it."

"I'm not making a big deal about it," Michel simpers, "because I knew it would happen. A blind man could see it."

"Huh," I huff out.

"Really?" Joslyn asks Michel curiously.

"Really," he affirms, and then turns to face us although he's all business as he speaks directly to Joslyn. "Now, I have to go over to wardrobe and make sure the costumes are ready. I'll be back in about fifteen to start your makeup so get in your robe."

"Yes, sir," she says with a mock salute, which makes me snort.

When Michel struts back out, I move to take Joslyn back in my arms, as I'd like to have one more kiss before her mom storms in on us. Instead, she holds her palms out to me and shakes her head.

"We don't have much time before Mom gets here," she whispers uncomfortably. "But I have to tell you something and it can't wait until after the show."

I go on hyper alert, every nerve in my body firing. Putting a hand to the back of her neck, I give her a gentle squeeze and try to keep the worry out of my tone. "What's wrong?"

Joslyn pulls my hand away from her neck by latching onto my wrist and leading me over to the small love seat. She sits down, pulling me along. I sit with enough distance between us that I can angle her way to look at her as she talks.

She worries at her bottom lip and can't seem to open up the conversation.

"Did something happen at dinner tonight with Ian?" I hazard a guess. Because that's the only major thing that's happened since we talked a few hours ago.

Joslyn head-bobs quickly in acknowledgment. "Yes. I signed his contract to represent me, then he had more documents for me to look at. A tentative offer to attach to a movie role provided I do well at the audition."

"A movie role?" I ask, perplexed. Joslyn's a singer. We've talked about her dreams and they never included acting.

"It's a role where the heroine is an aspiring singer and it's about her clawing her way to the top," she tells me. "It's supposedly gritty and heavy on drama."

"Can you act?" I inquire and realize that might be a shitty thing to ask, but I know Joslyn. She's critical of her own talents.

She gives me a look that tells me just how much I narrowed in on her worry. "No," she hisses at me in a low voice, I guess afraid her mom could be listening on the other side of the door or something. "I have no clue how to act. Never thought about it."

"Then why offer it to you?" I ask her, and then feel the need to amend. "Not that I don't think you could do anything you set your mind to, but this is huge, Joslyn. I mean really huge."

"I know," she says almost hysterically. "This isn't about surpassing my dreams. This is about being something I never even wanted before."

"Wow," I mutter as my mind starts to race.

"Justin Voss has already signed on," she says, her voice actually squeaking a bit in her distress.

I raise my eyebrows and shake my head.

She rolls her eyes. "Justin Voss. Only one of the hottest new actors out there."

"Cripes," I breathe out.

"What am I going to do?" Joslyn almost starts to cry and I pull her into me. "I can't act. I'll be a total failure. But Mom really wants me to do this and I don't want to let her down."

I give Joslyn a hard hug, but then I push her back so I can look at her face. I bend a little so I can peer right at her. "I'm quite sure you pointed out to Ian you've never acted before. What did he say?"

"He said he had Hollywood's best acting coach on standby to work with me and that he could tell by the way I handled myself on stage that I would have some basic acting skills I could easily develop. He didn't seem to think it was an issue."

My fear for Joslyn—stemming from her fear—recedes immediately. "Well, that's good. I mean, he has confidence in you. So it's probably nothing to worry about."

Her gaze drops from mine and I have to put my fingers under her chin to force her to look at me. "Talk to me. What's truly bothering you?"

She shakes her head like she can't bear to say the words, so I patiently wait. Finally, she lets out an exhale and unloads. "Yes, I'm wigged out they may want me for a big movie role and I have no clue if I'm any good at it. But more than anything, I don't feel ready for this. It's just moving so fast and I'm so overwhelmed."

"How soon do you have to decide?" I ask her.

"They want me in LA for an audition this weekend." Her face is awash with misery at the prospect. "And if I do good, they'll offer me the part. They apparently want me for my voice, but if I can act, it's mine."

"Wow," I say as I rub my hand over the back of my neck. It's a lot to take in.

"I've been going crazy waiting for you to get here so I could tell you. You have to tell me what to do, Kynan. I need someone objective because my mom is pushing me hard."

"You think I'm objective?" I ask her incredulously. Because the way I'm feeling right now, I want to pick her up, throw her over my shoulder, and carry her down to Mexico. I have enough money saved up from my days in the Royal Marines that we could buy a nice little hacienda and live happily ever after.

"Of course you're objective," she murmurs with a smile. "You're the most upstanding person I know."

I want to curse the heavens for giving me this amazing, complex woman who makes it so hard not to just fall deeply in love with her, as well as giving me a conscience where I can't put myself as the top priority in her life. I have to make sure she has good advice all the way around.

"I think you have to do the audition, Joslyn. If you don't, you'll always wonder at what might have been. And you have nothing to lose doing it. If you're bad, then you're bad, and you know your life will be as an amazing singer. Ian will have another opportunity for you. But if you're good, you may have stumbled onto something that you were meant to be and never even knew it."

Her eyes get shiny and her voice rasps when she says, "But I'm also supposed to be yours, and I have the feeling this is going to take that away."

"Never," I promise her, although I can't know that to be true. "But you can't worry about that right now. You have enough worries on your plate trying to figure out whether or not you can even act."

She snickers and then giggles, and the wetness leaves her eyes.

The door flies open and Michel comes back in, casting us a cursory glance. He snaps his fingers with impatience. "Robe. Get in your robe. We have lots to do to take your beauty to the stratosphere, darling."

Both Joslyn and I laugh and I give her a quick kiss on the mouth. "Get in your robe. I'm going to run out to get you a Frappuccino. I'll be back in a few."

"You are the best boyfriend ever," she exclaims and then kisses me not so briefly and a little bit hot. I groan and push her away. Michel watches and fans himself dramatically.

I leave the dressing room and head down a hall that will lead to the cast entrance/exit. Just as I'm opening the door to step out, Madeline is on the other side getting ready to enter.

We both startle in surprise, but I give her a smile. "Madeline... how are you?"

Her lips press into a flat line. "I wish I could say I was well, but you must know I'm not happy about this thing with you and Joslyn."

"I can only imagine," I reply dryly.

"She has big things ahead of her," she tells me pointedly. "Please don't be selfish and hold her back. Don't ruin this for her."

The crass Brit inside me would tell her exactly what to do with those sentiments but I have to remember this is Joslyn's mom and if I have anything to do with it, she's going to be in my life a long time.

"Madeline," I say in a warm, sincere voice. "I will only ever support Joslyn and that includes a career that might lead her away from here. You don't ever have to worry about it. Her success is more important to me than anything else."

She blinks at me in confusion, then her eyes narrow somewhat in distrust.

I nod and add on, "I even encouraged her to go for that movie audition. I think she'd be amazing."

Her eyes narrow further and she asks suspiciously, "You do?"

"I do," I tell her earnestly, but I also trust that Joslyn is going to be the one that makes the decision no matter what I or her mother wants. I vow to myself I'm going to make sure she relies on her own gut instinct, her own desires, and what she really wants out of life.

If I can ever do justice to my feelings for Joslyn, it will be to make sure she stays true to herself all the way and that she pursues the dreams she wants.

Regardless of how I or her mother feels about it.

Chapter 16

Joslyn

"I have faith in you," Justin whispers before he kisses me.

His lips are soft, his hands gentle on my face, but I can't get into it. My body is stiff as a board and my tongue is as dry as sandpaper.

Justin pulls away slightly to look in my eyes, and I see amusement there. And not the kind where we'd share a mutual laugh but more in a condescending way. He thinks I'm adorable for even trying to hang on par with someone of his caliber.

"Okay," Marshall King calls out to us and I take a big step back from Justin. "That was fine, Joslyn."

I expected him to yell "cut" but we're not filming so I guess that's not how it works. This is merely my audition for the movie "Shining Star," a drama about a poor girl from the wrong side of the tracks who makes it big on the talent of her amazing voice. The audition is taking place in a rented conference room in downtown LA and I've not felt comfortable since we got off the plane this morning.

I turn toward my mom to see her reaction and restrain myself from wiping my mouth. It felt weird to kiss another man, and although Kynan assured me he was okay with it because he knows the audition called for it, it still feels a little like betrayal.

My mom gives me an encouraging smile. Marshall, who is the casting director for the movie, stands from his chair at the end of the table and turns to Ian. He nods toward the door. "Let's talk."

Ian also gives me a smile intended to reassure, although I'm pretty sure I bombed this audition. The mere fact Marshall told me my performance was "fine" is validation.

When the door shuts behind them, Justin turns to me. I thought I'd be star struck by him as he's one of the hottest young actors out there but instead I was just a bit disgusted. He might have the dark dreamy looks every girl fantasizes about, but his personality turned me off from the start. Vain, entitled, and slightly rude, I was bordering on being repulsed.

He ordered one of Marshall's assistants to bring him a very specific brand of vitamin water and when she told him they didn't have any, he ordered her to go get it. He then shot me a leering grin as if his power would impress me. I glared at him in return.

"They're not going to offer you the part," he says and the negative words out of the blue cause me to jump.

My mother's eyebrows knit together. "Why is that?" she asks in a neutral voice but I can hear the slight panic within.

Justin gives me his back to regard my mother with even more amusement. "Because her delivery is stilted and she kisses with all the passion of a dead fish. She'll never be able to sell herself to an audience."

Rude as hell.

There's no response my mother can give because this is THE Justin Voss telling her critical information that's probably very accurate. We know nothing of the business and he knows everything.

Pivoting my way, he gives me a smile that doesn't reach his eyes. "Well, it's been... charming. Best of luck to you in life."

Without another word, he casually saunters out the door and it's then that I notice that he never even opened the bottle of water he made that poor assistant go out for.

When the door closes, I mutter, "What a douche."

"That's Hollywood, I suppose," my mom replies and doesn't seem put out in the slightest.

"You really think that's how it is here?" Because if it is, I hate it already.

She shrugs. "I guess it's like this anywhere. There are nice people and there are jerks. You just have to learn to let it roll off your back."

I suppose that's good advice but it's hard. I take things to heart and I don't doubt everything Justin just said—right down to my dead fish kiss—was true. I was awful but I don't know what the hell I'm doing. The few days I had with an acting coach in Vegas weren't very fruitful at all. I tried to give the delivery like I was instructed but it was hard when you constantly doubt yourself. Or when you're just not feeling it.

That's part of the problem. I'm pursuing something that was never even on my radar. I'm having a hard time drumming up an internal passion for this type of art.

God bless Kynan this past week. We settled into a routine that had me walking on clouds. He had to work during the day so I practiced with the acting coach. He'd come see my show and after, he'd take me out for a late meal. Then it was back to his apartment where he would make love to me, sometimes twice, before we'd lapse into long talks about our future.

I never stayed all night. He usually brought me home sometime after midnight, with the new bodyguard, Cash, awkwardly following behind. My mother never waited up for me but I could tell by her disapproving look the next morning she didn't like me spending time at Kynan's. Not because of my age, because my mom already respected me as an adult I believe, but because I was spending too much time with him.

On my two days off this past week, I met Kynan at his place after he got off work and he helped me practice the scenes I was auditioning for. He was patient and encouraging, and totally hilarious as he tried to "play" Justin's part in the movie. When we got to the kiss part, it was usually all over for both of us. We ended up naked and rolling around wherever we happened to be. That's how we ended up christening his couch and kitchen table.

And oh my... the sex.

I feel like I've turned into such a slut with wanting him all the time. I could be in the middle of a show, happen to turn to glance at him off stage, and my body reacts. One time my nipples went painfully hard and were popping through my costume. I was embarrassed but still incredibly turned on with wanting him when the show ended. We hurried out of the theater that night without taking off my makeup.

I fondled him on the drive home, almost making him wreck. When we got into his apartment, I dropped to my knees before he even got the door closed and started unzipping his jeans. It was the first time I had him in my mouth and I'll never forget the sounds I pulled from him that night.

"What are you thinking about?" my mom asks, and my cheeks flame hot that she busted me fantasizing about Kynan.

So I lie to her. "I was just thinking that if I can't get through a kiss with Justin, how am I going to do the sex scenes?"

That's another issue I have with the script. There are two pretty explicit scenes, and while Ian assured me he could put in a no-nudity clause, I really didn't think I could act my way through it. One of the scenes would be me and Justin having sex up against a wall where he would be pounding ruthlessly inside of me. I'd be clothed but I'd have to put on quite a show and it made me slightly nauseated to think about it.

"I suspect part of the problem is that man," she says disapprovingly.

"His name is Kynan and you're well aware of that," I drawl. But I don't deny what she says. Part of the problem is that I don't want to be kissing or simulating sex with anyone other than Kynan.

"Well, regardless of the problem, for the type of money you'll make, you're going to have to find a way to get past it," she reminds me.

"If they offer me the part," I retort, because she knows as well as I do that I did not do well in this audition.

That causes her mouth to snap shut because she knows I'm right. For the first time since she's been managing me, I've not performed with stellar perfection.

The door opens up and Ian walks in. He looks neither upset nor happy, merely resigned. Motioning to the seats at the table, he makes a silent request for us to sit down. He takes a chair and clasps his hands on the table. "Okay... the good news. They love your voice. They feel it's perfect for the movie and you bring passion to the songs that the other actresses auditioning can't pull off."

"And the bad news?" my mother clips out, eager to get to the heart of the matter.

"She didn't carry the dialogue and that kiss was atrocious," he replies bluntly.

Even though I knew all that to be true, I still flinch from the criticism. However, as much as that hurt to hear, I'm slightly relieved to be cut loose.

"More good news though," Ian continues and my stomach pitches. "They think you can improve. Now that they see what the problems are, they want you to work with a different acting coach. They'll give you a new audition in two weeks. You'll have to move here immediately as some of the scenes they will want you to work are with Justin and he's filming here now."

"No," I say without thought.

"We'll do it," my mother says right on the heels of my words.

We both turn to look at each other and I seize the opportunity to draw my line. "I'm not leaving my show. I have people that have advanced ticket purchases."

"They can be refunded," my mom says with a careless wave of her hand.

"No," I reply again, and then turn to Ian. "I'll do another audition and I'll practice. But it has to be in Vegas so I can continue to work."

"And see that man," my mom mutters.

My head whips toward her and I glare. "For once, you're wrong. I am only thinking about not letting people down who want to come see the show."

"Those people are strangers to you, Joslyn," my mother replies with a responding glare. "You cannot waste an opportunity like this on nameless, faceless people."

"Ladies," Ian says in a soothing tone. "I'm sure we can compromise."

Our heads turn his way, but Ian only looks at my mother because he likes dealing with her. "Maddie... I'm sure we can get the acting coach down to Vegas, and we'll just have to work around not having Justin to do scenes with her. In fact, perhaps her... boyfriend can help."

"He can," I blurt and it sounds way too excited and immature.

Ian shoots me a patronizing smile, then looks back to my mom. "It will be fine. I promise."

He gets a tremulous attempt at a return smile but I can see my mother is feeling out of control.

Join the crowd, Mom.

Join the crowd.

Chapter 17

Kynan

"You can do this, Julie," I drawl in overexaggerated enthusiasm as I read from the manuscript for *Shining Star*. "You've already sung your way into my heart and I know you can do it to theirs."

Joslyn bites her bottom lip, trying not to snicker at me. I cock an eyebrow at her and she starts to laugh. She falls from her position, sitting naked and cross legged against the headboard of my bed, landing on her side. She's adorable in that she makes sure to hold the sheet over her breasts, despite the fact I know every inch of her body.

Hell, I've licked every inch of it.

I just stare at her in amusement, but it's no chore to do this. I could stare at her for every minute of every day.

I'm on the opposite end of the bed, in my boxer briefs and propped on my side on a pillow while she laughs. It's a beautiful sound and makes me want to fuck her again.

And again.

And again.

Instead, I chide her. "You're not taking this seriously. And you're not projecting like you're supposed to."

She stops laughing, those blue eyes just pinned on me blankly.

I grin at her and mimic her acting coach, who sounds like he should be narrating Masterpiece Theater. "You must speak from the diaphragm and project."

She starts laughing again so hard, she's wiping tears out of her eyes. Not that she'd see it, but I roll my eyes before lunging across the bed for her. Within moments, I have my back against the hardboard and her body cradled in my lap, the round curves of her ass pressing down on my hard-on.

But I don't act on it.

Tiling my head, I rest my temple against the top of her head. "I know you don't like doing this stuff but it's important. And you're really getting good at it."

"Really?" she asks as she draws lazy patterns on my chest with her fingertips. "Because every time I try these lines, I feel nothing but frustration over how hard it is for me to do it well."

I give her a squeeze. "Singing comes so naturally to you, I imagine it is hard to struggle at something like this."

She draws back to look at me, an irritated expression on her face. "And why am I even doing this? To work on a movie with a rude, arrogant star who I just know will make my life miserable. To suffer the patronizing way Ian talks to me and my mother's ruthlessness to see me rise to the top."

"You're doing it because this could set up a career you never even dreamed of having," I remind her solemnly. We've had this conversation many times the past several days.

"Why do you have to be so adult?" she mutters and I can't help but chuckle.

My hand slides up her side, under her breast where I test its weight. I give it a soft squeeze and whisper, "You are all adult, Joslyn. Don't doubt yourself."

Her breath hitches but I release her and go back to the conversation at hand because it's important. But first, I try to lighten the mood. "Well, I for one am glad Justin is rude. That way you won't fall for him."

Joslyn snorts. "As if. He's such a jerk I can barely stand to kiss him."

I grimace and pull her in tight to me. "Yeah... let's not talk about that part of the movie. I'd just as soon ignore the fact another man is going to have his mouth on you."

Joslyn pulls away to look at me earnestly. "I won't do it if it bothers you."

I smile and shake my head. "You may choose not to do this movie, but don't ever make that decision based on whether or not the scenes cause you to touch another dude. That's got nothing to do with me and you and I can separate out in my mind that it's acting. Okay?"

"Okay," she murmurs but adds on, "but I just am not sure if I should be doing this. There's something that's not sitting right with me."

"Is it because you're afraid for us or are you really just not liking this?"

Her expression turns to chagrin. "A lot of it is because I'm afraid of what will happen to us if I have to leave, but a large part of it is that I'm just not feeling that same rush of joy doing this as I do with singing. In fact, I'm not feeling anything at all. It's like I was working a job as a secretary or something. Glad to have the work but at the end of the day, I'd rather be doing something more fulfilling."

I find that to be very telling and this doesn't surprise me. Every time she has to meet with her acting coach, she turns glum. When I try to practice with her, she fights me on it. I thought it might be her nerves and she's trying to lower her own expectations of herself, but I'm starting to see that she just doesn't have a burning need to be an actor.

Not the way she lives and breathes for her music.

"I never wanted this," she tells me in a low voice, almost as if she's ashamed. "I almost feel like my mom has lost sight of my dreams and she's pursuing hers."

I think Joslyn might be right about that and I think her insight is pretty accurate from what I've been able to observe, but I don't validate.

I can't.

I simply can't do anything that will turn her away from doing this audition. I can't be any part of such a decision that could make her hate me one day if she has regrets. So even though inside I'm terrified of what will happen to us once she leaves, I can't let her know that.

If she's offered the part, the filming is beginning very soon on the East Coast. It's projected to take three months and, while I could wait until the end of time for her, I wouldn't be human if I didn't admit I've got some doubts as to whether we can survive as a couple in that time period. She'll be surrounded by famous people and leading an exciting life. She could very well decide that she doesn't have room for a relationship. I'm smart enough to know that even though what we have is so fucking real, it doesn't mean it's not fragile. If we don't foster this, it could die and it's sure as hell going to be hard to nurture what we have if we aren't physically together.

So I remain encouraging and supportive despite my misgivings, and that's the way it will be.

"This may not have been your dream before, but it doesn't mean it can't be your dream now," I tell her, just as I've practiced in my head over and over again so I can really sell my support to her. "This is a very rare opportunity, Jos. Forget about the money you could make and think about the amount of contacts you'll come out of this with. Or the exposure. You'll have record labels lined up around the block to sign you."

None of this seems to matter to Joslyn. She leans in close to me and whispers, "Promise you'll wait for me and that you won't fall madly in love with the first pretty girl that catches your eye if I get the part."

Funny that she's the one that needs assurance. I could easily ask the same of her, but I'm too much of a man to admit my vulnerability to her. "There's no way that could ever happen. You're it for me, Joslyn."

"You're it for me too," she replies and then presses her mouth to mine.

And as expected, my body reacts. How could it not when she's warm, naked, and sitting in my lap? I put a palm to her breast and squeeze it as we kiss. Her nipples are so sensitive they harden upon contact. She wiggles and shifts around, causing painfully delicious friction on my dick.

My hand slides from her breast, down her stomach, and in between her legs, which part for me. I flick at her clit, causing her to writhe with need. I press fingers into her and slowly thrust them in and out until she's all but begging for me to let her come.

"I want to ride you," she pants and doesn't give me a chance to deny her.

Not that I would.

Before I can even move my hand from her sweet spot, she's flipping on my lap and straddling my groin. I scoot down from the headboard, bringing her right along with me, until I'm lying flat and she's sitting on me with her legs spread wide.

I take a moment just to look at her nakedness and the fact that sometimes she can be painfully shy in her nudity, but other times she'll just open right up for me.

This is one of those times.

We had a "talk" earlier this week about safe sex, and after mutual assurances and praise be to birth control pills, we decided to do away with condoms. It's something that is sacred to me as I've never not used a condom. Never been with a woman long enough or cared about one enough to even have that conversation. While I've been with many, I've always been protected and was up to date on my health screenings. In all her sweetness, Joslyn told me she'd only been with one other guy when she lost her virginity and they used a condom then. It was enough for me to do away with the damn things and let me just say... fucking my girl bare is probably the best thing I've ever felt in my life.

Joslyn shifts and presses her knees into the mattress, rising up. I use the opportunity to push my briefs down and free myself. She bats my hand away to take my length in her tiny palm. I groan as she squeezes but keep my eyes open so I can watch how she feeds me into her body.

Christ, I see stars in my eyes as she takes me in and swallows me into heat and wetness, and I want to thrust up into her so bad, but I also want her to fuck me.

I grit my teeth and raise my hands up to tuck them beneath my head. I clasp them hard and tell myself to leave them there so I don't take the control away from Joslyn.

She stares down at me with hazy eyes, as if she doesn't know what to do for a moment. But I know she does because she's ridden me before. In fact, there's not a position we haven't tried.

Pressing her hands onto my abs, she gains her center and rotates her hips a little.

"Mmm," she purrs and licks her bottom lip.

Fuck, that's sexy.

Joslyn rises like a siren moving from ocean to air, letting me slide free almost to the tip before she pushes back down onto me.

Fuck yes, that's how I like it.

Now digging her teeth down into her bottom lip and a fierce look of determination, Joslyn starts to fuck me. Slowly at first, but as her own need builds, she picks up the pace. I love watching her chase an orgasm. The other night I made her masturbate while I watched and it may have been the hottest thing I've ever seen.

"Touch yourself," I tell her through gritted teeth.

She does, using one hand to rub her clit and the other to pinch her nipple. It's so damn erotic I can feel myself starting to crest.

"Come on, baby," I urge and her hand moves faster between her legs. I know it feels damn good to her because she starts to falter on her rhythm.

Fuck it. My hands go to her hips and I help her along. I force her to move faster on me, using my strength to guide her up and down. She works at her slippery core and when she cries out, tightening all around me in release, I lose my shit and start to come right along with her. I bark out a cry of satisfaction, using my hands to keep her pressed onto me tight even as my hips buck upward. She shudders and I pulse inside her, and I've never felt closer to another human before as our orgasms ripple, then mingle together.

Joslyn collapses onto my chest and I rub my hands along her sweaty back, giving her whispers of praise for rocking my world.

Goddamn, she rocks my world.

I'm going to be crushed when she leaves.

Chapter 18

Joslyn

I put forth every ounce of effort into pretending Justin Voss is my Kynan as we engage in the scene-ending kiss. Amazingly, my stomach doesn't churn and for even a brief moment, I'm lost in thinking about Kynan. He drove me and Mom to the airport early this morning for our flight to Los Angeles, giving me a hard hug at the terminal.

"Try your best, babe," he told me. "That's all you can do. But no matter what happens, I'm so damn proud of you."

That has stuck with me all day. Through the flight and car ride over to the same conference room where I had my first audition. It bolstered me when Justin made some disparaging remarks about my abilities to the casting director, not even caring that I could hear him. It pushed me right through my fear when it was time to perform.

Justin pulls away from me and leers. "Damn, Joslyn. You clearly learned how to kiss these past few weeks."

"I just pretended you were my boyfriend," I reply sweetly but in a low tone only he could hear. He gives me a smirk to indicate he doesn't believe me or perhaps it's that he doesn't care.

"You nailed it," Marshall says with a huge grin on his face. He stands up from the chair and gives me a slow clap of appreciation, which embarrasses the hell out of me. Ian and my mom are smiling even more widely than Marshall, and I can see at least their dreams are probably coming true. "You really worked hard these past few weeks, Joslyn. I'm so impressed."

Marshall then turns to Ian. "I want her. The proposed terms we discussed before the first audition still stand if you want the part."

It's disconcerting the way they are talking about me as if I'm a piece of meat at auction. None of it is addressed to me. It's "I want *her*" and he says to Ian "if *you* want the part." I want to say, *Hey... wait a minute. Maybe someone should ask me.*

But I don't.

Because why bother? They wouldn't listen to me anyway.

Marshall and Ian shake on the deal. Justin leaves without a word. Marshall walks out without even acknowledging me, only calling out to Ian, "I'm calling my assistant right now to email you the contract ASAP."

When the conference room door closes, Ian holds his arms out with a shit-eating grin on his face directed solely at my mother. "What did I tell you, Maddie? I knew she could do it."

"So did I," she replies back with smug confidence. And then as an afterthought, she turns to me. "You did great, honey."

Gee, thanks.

"Let's sit down and talk about some minor details that we could probably get added to the contract when he sends the first draft over." Ian pulls out a chair for my mom, and then gives me a sideways glance. "Joslyn... if you want to run out for a coffee or something while we work, there's a little shop just down the block."

"That's a great idea," my mom says as she beams at me. "Bring us all back some coffee."

My return smile is over-exaggerated. "Sure. Be glad to."

But I'm already forgotten as Ian and my mom huddle together with dollar signs in their eyes. I turn and walk out of the conference room, down the hallway, and straight into the bathroom, which is miraculously empty.

I pull out my phone and call Kynan.

He answers almost immediately. "Well?" he asks in a hesitant tone.

"Looks like I've got the part," I say glumly.

Rather than a burst of congratulations, Kynan adjusts his tone to react accordingly to mine. "What's wrong, Jos? You should be happy right now."

"Then tell me why I'm not," I say softly.

He's silent and I wait.

More silence.

"Kynan?" I say tentatively.

"You accomplished your goal," he finally says neutrally. "Now you have to ask yourself, do you want to accomplish the next one? You got the part, now do you want to push forward and make the movie? My advice stands the same, Joslyn. Make sure that whatever you do, you do it without regret."

"What do you think I should do?" I ask him, because it's clear he's not willing to stake a contrary position just now.

"I want you to do what makes you happiest," he says without hesitation but it's still a hedge. "You do what's best for you. Not me, not your mom, not Ian. Figure out what is best for you, and you take control of your life. The only thing I will say with complete surety is that if you want this movie, then you have my full support. I'll wait for you no matter how long you're gone from me."

If I thought his words would help push me in one direction or another, I'd be wrong. He's telling me nothing he hadn't already reiterated this past week as he helped me practice.

And I get it. Kynan is giving me the room to control my destiny. He, more than anyone, recognizes how little control I've had in my life, and if there's a time to take it back, it's now.

"I've got to go," I say, almost absently, to Kynan.

"You okay?" he asks.

"Yeah... I've got to go get some coffees for everyone. I'll call you a bit later."

"Okay," he says and I hear the worry in his voice. It's the sweetest sound, knowing he has my back.

"I miss you," I tell him.

"Miss you more," he reassures me and then disconnects.

I take my time walking out of the office building. I purposely turn the wrong way from the coffee shop, taking a walk around the entire block to give myself time to think. I eventually get a latte for me and two black coffees for my mom and Ian, not knowing what he likes.

Not caring either, as I've got more important things on my mind.

When I push the door of the conference room open, Mom and Ian are in the same spot except they have his laptop open in front of them. She glances up and smiles. "Oh, honey... I'm glad you're here. We have to decide on some extras we want built into the contract. They're going to arrange for a place for you to stay near filming but we believe it's better to ask for a per diem amount so we can choose where we want to stay. And Ian feels the royalty—"

"I need to talk with you privately," I tell my mother, raising my voice enough to catch her attention.

She goes mute and just blinks at me.

I move my attention to Ian. "If you don't mind excusing us."

Ian doesn't respond but turns to look at my mother for permission. She in turn looks back to me. "Can't this wait? We have important things to work on."

My reply is simple. "No. It can't wait."

Mom's lips press into a flat grimace and her voice is tight. "Ian... if you don't mind excusing us for just a moment. I'm sure this won't take long."

Ian is slow to rise, as if he's waiting for me to change my mind and just give up on my desire to speak my mind. I stare resolutely at him as he makes his exit.

When the door closes, I take the seat he vacated and angle it to face my mother. "I'm having major doubts about taking this offer."

My mom laughs. "That's my girl, always wanting the best deal. But Ian assures me what they're offering is fair for the industry."

I take a breath and shake my head. "No. I am having doubts about accepting at all. I don't think I want to do this."

I get no validation back. Instead, my mother scoffs with an impatient wave of her hand—it's her trademark move to indicate what I've said has no merit to her. "Don't be ridiculous, Joslyn. This is the offer of a lifetime. You'd be stupid not to take it. Now, we need to decide—"

"Mother," I snap in a brittle voice to get her attention.

She goes rigid and her eyes go wide with shock.

"I need to have a mother/daughter talk with you," I say in a gentler tone. "I need you to put aside being my business manager and I need you to listen to my worries only as my mother."

Her face registers nothing back to me. It's as if I just spoke to her in a foreign language. Has she forgotten completely how to be my mom?

And why did I not do something to change this earlier?

"Mom, please," I beg her.

Another moment of blank indifference before she sighs, setting back in her chair. "Okay. I'm listening."

While I doubt she's listening the way I need her to, I use the opportunity to tell her my concerns. "You know I appreciate everything you do for me, but doing this movie is just not feeling right to me. I mean... when I step out on stage to sing, I might be sick with nerves, yet I feel like I'm supposed to be there. The joy I get is indescribable. It's what I'm supposed to do with my life."

I find not an ounce of empathy in her expression, but still, I push forward. "While this opportunity is a once in a lifetime thing—which I truly understand and appreciate—it's not an opportunity that excites me. It feels...wrong to me."

"How can you know that?" she asks as she leans forward. "You haven't even tried it yet. You could get on that movie set and just love it."

"Or I could be committing myself to months of misery," I counter.

My mother seems to consider this. She scoots her chair closer to mine and takes my hands. It's the first motherly move she's made and it bolsters me.

"Tell me truthfully," she says in a gentle tone. "How much of this is because you don't want to leave Kynan?"

I shake my head in frustration that she is so easily dismissing my concerns. "It's not about him. Yes, I'll miss him but he's going to wait for me. He's been supportive of me doing this."

My mom cocks a skeptical eyebrow.

I squeeze her hands. "He's only ever pushed me to go for this. He doesn't want me to have regrets."

Pulling her hands from mine, my mom seizes on the Kynan bandwagon. "Then I think you should listen to him. It sounds like wise advice indeed."

I growl in frustration, curling my hands into fists. "You're not even listening to me. I am telling you I don't want this. I know *you* want it, but I don't. I don't want to be an actress. I just want to sing."

"But when you sing, you are being an actress," my mom counters, her eyes shining bright. "Every time you step out on that stage, you are acting a role. Sure, you're singing and your voice is a natural talent, but you are selling yourself to that audience. And fine... you don't want to be an actress. I accept that. But why not do this one movie, which will undoubtedly lead you to sign with a record label much faster than we can get you there on your Vegas laurels?"

Ugh, I hate that that makes sense. I hate that she actually just validated my feelings like I wanted her to but provided me with a reasonable solution. Take this job, suffer the short term, and have the career of my dreams after.

"Trust me," my mother murmurs, putting her hands on my shoulders. "I only ever want what's best for you, and I think this will get you to where you want to be."

I really, really want to believe her. She's my mother and there's no reason not to.

Chapter 19

Kynan

I feel only slightly guilty that I'm playing Solitaire on my phone rather than reviewing the packet of materials Jerico handed me earlier today. He's taking on our first government contract and while it's not high-speed black ops type of work, it does involve some sneaky-ass human intelligence gathering in a foreign country filled with sand.

It's way more exciting than working casino security, but that job is almost wrapped up. We have some sub-contractors in now doing installation on new surveillance equipment. When that's done, we'll do staff training with implementation of new security procedures our company formulated, and when that's done... well, we're done.

Jerico has been busy drumming up new work. He's got several private residences under contract for new security systems, and when I say residences, I mean mega-mansions from Texas westward. He's also set up some private bodyguard work for some politicians in DC and one country music singer in Nashville.

All in all, it seems that his company is going to be a huge success if evidenced by the rate at which he is bringing legitimate business into the fold.

I glance at the binder sitting on my desk, knowing I should quit procrastinating and read it. Jerico says it provides the mission objectives as well as his plan to accomplish them. He wants me to review, tear it up if necessary, and make it better.

And I will.

As soon as I hear from Joslyn.

She did not sound good when I talked to her after the audition this morning. That was several hours ago and I've not heard anything since. I only can assume that she, her mother, and Ian might be out celebrating. Or maybe they're still ironing out details.

There's a knock on my door which I closed so I could play Solitaire without anyone noticing. My office is about the size of a broom closet but I told Jerico that I didn't want one. He insisted, so I told him to give me the smallest one as I wouldn't be in it much. I much preferred being out in the field.

I place my phone upside down on my desk and say, "Come in."

Jerico peeks his head inside and smiles at me. His gaze goes to the binder then back to me. "So... what did you think?"

"Haven't read it yet," I tell him.

He appraises me and his smile turns into a smirk. He steps into my office, walks up to my desk, and takes my phone. Turning it over, he sees the half-finished game of Solitaire.

His eyes flash with mischief. "Knew it. You always played games on your phone when you were troubled."

I should be irritated that he knows me so well but, in all actuality, I'm grateful I don't have to explain my lackadaisical attitude toward a project he asked me to review.

So I just shrug in response.

"Have you heard anything more?" he asks me. He stopped by earlier after I'd talked to Joslyn, and I told him she'd been offered the part.

I shake my head. "I guess they're ironing out details or something."

"Why don't you call her?" he suggests.

I glare at him. "And what... look like a pussy?"

"You *are* a pussy," he says with a laugh. "This girl has you twisted up. Never thought I'd see the mighty Kynan McGrath fall to a wisp of a girl."

Woman, but not going to argue with him.

His gaze goes back to the binder. "I really need your eyes on it. I could give it to someone else but would rather you do this with me."

He's not talking about the review. He's talking about the entire mission and I have to admit, I'm feeling so out of sorts, I'd love nothing more than to head off to Afghanistan or Syria or wherever they're calling for our help. I'd love to just hang out there while Joslyn is filming her movie, so at least I can be so focused on something vital and probably dangerous, which means I wouldn't be mooning over her too badly.

I take the binder in hand. "I'll start it now."

Jerico nods with a smile. "Thanks, buddy. Let me know what you think when you're done."

He turns to walk out of my office, only to be brought up short by August Greenfield. He's a new hire, straight from the Las Vegas PD and since he's the newest, he has "front desk" duty. We still haven't hired a full-time receptionist and until then, the newer employees are taking turns to catch any walk-in traffic.

August peeks his head around Jerico. "You got someone in the lobby to see you."

A jolt of awareness pulses through my body. "Who?"

He shrugs. "Some blonde woman."

"In the future," Jerico says blandly, "you really should try to get visitors' names."

August blushes and I push up from my desk.

Blonde woman.

Can only be one person that I know with blonde hair.

At least I hope.

Without a word acknowledging the two men standing there, I scramble up from my desk and rush past them. Down the hall, forsaking the elevator and taking the fire stairwell three steps at a time to the first floor.

I come bursting out the door, skid across the marble floor, and come to a rigid stop as I take in Joslyn standing there with her suitcase clutched in front of her with both hands.

It tells me everything I need to know.

"You're not doing the movie," I breathe out, and it is an exhale of pure relief. I didn't realize how much I was dreading her leaving until that very moment.

She gives me a smile. "My mom is kind of pissed at me right now. I kind of need a place to stay."

My strides aren't nearly long enough to take me to her but I cover the lobby in just two and a half. I remove the suitcase from her clutches, drop it carelessly to the side, and frame her face with my hands. "You're staying?"

"I'm staying," she affirms. "I just—"

Her words are cut off with my mouth on hers and I almost bend her backward in half as I lean into the kiss to give it all my worth.

One of her hands slides into my hair and the other to my shoulder, and she gives it back to me just as good.

When I'm out of oxygen and filled with curiosity again, I pull away from her and just take her in. She's even more beautiful than I remember and she's been gone less than a day.

Taking her by the hand, I lead her over to a leather couch that I don't think has been sat on yet. We take a seat side by side, and she angles in toward me. Her expression is distressed, the corners of her mouth drawn downward. "It was awful," she says quietly and looks down at her hands resting in her lap. "It was the worst fight I've ever had with my mother."

"Start from the beginning," I tell her as I take her hands and give a squeeze. "Deep breath and tell me all of it."

She inhales deeply, her nostrils flaring. The rush of air coming out is slow and steady and I get a brave smile from her. "I just couldn't do it, Kynan. I know it might be career suicide and I know I may be passing up the opportunity of a lifetime, but I could not commit myself to something that I know I would hate with a passion. My career is supposed to fulfill me and this wouldn't. I just know it deep in my heart, and no matter how much you or anyone else told me to go for it, I just couldn't."

"It's okay," I reassure her. "I told you to do what was best for you and you did. But I'm sure as fuck happy for myself."

That gets a tiny mirthless laugh from Joslyn as her expression turns grim once again. "I don't think my mom is ever going to talk to me again. Of course, she blames it all on you. Thinks the only reason I'm doing this is to stay with you."

"Is there any part of that statement that's true?" I ask curiously, because I'm damn proud right now that Joslyn made a business decision all on her own that was in her personal best interest.

I see a tinge of chagrin in her eyes. "Maybe a little. I mean... the part I said I'd hate it with a passion took into consideration that part of what I'd hate is being away from you. I know that might be stupid and immature—"

"Don't," I say gruffly, taking her chin in my hand. "Don't put yourself down like that. I think you made a decision that was incredibly difficult and I don't think you did it flippantly. If you had wanted it, you'd have gone for it."

"Would I?" she asks skeptically.

"Let me ask you this... if you'd been giving a great recording contract and had to go halfway around the world to cut an album, and it would take you away from me for an extended period of time, would you do it?"

She considers, nibbling on her lower lip. Fuck if I don't want to nibble there, but that will come later.

She finally nods. "I think so. I mean, if the offer was right."

"Then stop worrying about if you made a silly decision based on love," I tell her.

She blinks at me. "Love?"

"I love you," I tell her simply. "And you love me too. Frankly, we're kind of barmy arses not to have said it to each other yet. I figure you have enough on your mind and have been worried about all this bloody movie stuff, I thought I'd make the declaration of love first. Sort of take the pressure off you."

"You're oh so kind," she drawls sarcastically then she gasps as I pull her to me for a hard kiss.

When we break, her eyes go soft. "I love you. More than I ever knew was possible."

"Same here, Jos. What we have here is the real opportunity of a lifetime. I'm glad neither one of us is going to let it pass us by."

"So I can move in with you?" she asks with a dimpled grin.

I stand up from the couch, drawing her up with me. "Yes. In fact, let's go move you in right now."

Because I think we should re-christen my bed as now belonging fully to both me and Joslyn. I lead her back to where I dropped her suitcase and nab it from the floor. I get halfway to the door when I hear Jerico calling me.

"Taking the rest of the day off?" he asks slyly.

I look over my shoulder, see him exiting the elevator. "Yup. I'll be in tomorrow and will get right on that project."

He waves me off, shaking his head with amusement. "Bright and early," he commands.

"Bright and early," I acknowledge. And I'll be eager to hit the day running, because my life just started for real.

With my love.

My Joslyn.

Epilogue

This was no joyous homecoming. When Madeline Meyers opened the door to her darkened apartment, her shoulders were sagging with weariness and her heart was heavy.

It was also very angry.

How dare she do this to me? she seethed inwardly.

Dropping her rolling suitcase in the foyer, she kicked off her shoes and shut the door, not even bothering to turn the lock. She was far too preoccupied.

Grabbing her phone from her purse, she dialed Ian McMichaels because she was dying to see what he'd accomplished since she left L.A. a few hours ago.

Answering on the second ring, he started filling her in without them even exchanging a greeting.

Madeline listened and the more she listened, the lighter her shoulders felt. Ian was going to have no problem procuring what she needed to set things right. It would take a few days, but that was okay. Ian was stalling on the movie deal offer so they had time.

Smiling to herself, she started making a mental list of the things that needed to be done. By the time she hung up with Ian, she was practically walking on cloud nine.

Joslyn was going to do that movie. She just didn't know it yet.

Sign up for the 1001 Dark Nights Newsletter
and be entered to win a Tiffany Lock necklace.

There's a contest every quarter!

Go to www.1001DarkNights.com to subscribe.

As a bonus, all subscribers can download FIVE FREE exclusive
books!

Discover the Kristen Proby Crossover Collection

Soaring with Fallon: A Big Sky Novel
By Kristen Proby

Fallon McCarthy has climbed the corporate ladder. She's had the office with the view, the staff, and the plaque on her door. The unexpected loss of her grandmother taught her that there's more to life than meetings and conference calls, so she quit, and is happy to be a nomad, checking off items on her bucket list as she takes jobs teaching yoga in each place she lands in. She's happy being free, and has no interest in being tied down.

When Noah King gets the call that an eagle has been injured, he's not expecting to find a beautiful stranger standing vigil when he arrives. Rehabilitating birds of prey is Noah's passion, it's what he lives for, and he doesn't have time for a nosy woman who's suddenly taken an interest in Spread Your Wings sanctuary.

But Fallon's gentle nature, and the way she makes him laugh, and *feel* again draws him in. When it comes time for Fallon to move on, will Noah's love be enough for her to stay, or will he have to find the strength to let her fly?

* * * *

Wicked Force: A Wicked Horse Vegas/Big Sky Novella
By Sawyer Bennett

From *New York Times* and *USA Today* bestselling author Sawyer Bennett...

Joslyn Meyers has taken the celebrity world by storm, drawing the attention of millions. But one fan's affections has gone too far, and she's running to the one place she hopes he'll never find her – back home to Cunningham Falls.

Kynan McGrath leads The Jameson Group, a world-class security organization, and he's ready to do what it takes to keep Joslyn safe, even if it means giving up his own life in return. The one thing he's not prepared to lose, though, is his heart.

* * * *

Crazy Imperfect Love: A Dirty Dicks/Big Sky Novella
By KL Grayson

From *USA Today* bestselling author KL Grayson…

Abigail Darwin needs one thing in life: consistency. Okay, make that two things: consistency and order. Tired of being shackled to her obsessive-compulsive mind, Abigail is determined to break free. Which is why she's shaking things up.

Fresh out of nursing school, she takes a traveling nurse position. A new job in a new city every few months? That's a sure-fire way to keep her from settling down and falling into old habits. First stop, Cunningham Falls, Montana.

The only problem? She didn't plan on falling in love with the quaint little town, and she sure as heck didn't plan on falling for its resident surgeon, Dr. Drake Merritt

Laid back, messy, and spontaneous, Drake is everything she's not. But he is completely smitten by the new, quirky nurse working on the med-surg floor of the hospital.

Abby puts up a good fight, but Drake is determined to break through her carefully erected walls to find out what makes her tick. And sigh and moan and smile and laugh. Because he really loves her laugh.

But falling in love isn't part of Abby's plan. Will Drake have what it takes to convince her that the best things in life come from doing what scares us the most?

* * * *

Worth Fighting For: A Warrior Fight Club/Big Sky Novella
By Laura Kaye

From *New York Times* and *USA Today* bestselling author Laura Kaye…

Getting in deep has never felt this good…

Commercial diving instructor Tara Hunter nearly lost everything in an accident that saw her medically discharged from the navy. With the help of the Warrior Fight Club, she's fought hard to overcome her fears and get back in the water where she's always felt most at home. At work, she's tough, serious, and doesn't tolerate distractions. Which is why finding her gorgeous one-night stand on her new dive team is such a problem.

Former navy deep-sea diver Jesse Anderson just can't seem to stop making mistakes—the latest being the hot-as-hell night he'd spent with his new partner. This job is his second chance, and Jesse knows he shouldn't mix business with pleasure. But spending every day with Tara's smart mouth and sexy curves makes her so damn hard to resist.

Joining a wounded warrior MMA training program seems like the perfect way to blow off steam—until Jesse finds that Tara belongs too. Now they're getting in deep and taking each other down day and night, and even though it breaks all the rules, their inescapable attraction might just be the only thing truly worth fighting for.

* * * *

Nothing Without You: A Forever Yours/Big Sky Novella
By Monica Murphy

From *New York Times* and *USA Today* bestselling author Monica Murphy…

Designing wedding cakes is Maisey Henderson's passion. She puts her heart and soul into every cake she makes, especially since she's such a believer in true love. But then Tucker McCloud rolls back into town, reminding her that love is a complete joke. The pro football player is the hottest thing to come out of Cunningham Falls—and the boy who broke Maisey's heart back in high school.

He claims he wants another chance. She says absolutely not. But Maisey's refusal is the ultimate challenge to Tucker. Life is a game, and Tucker's playing to win Maisey's heart—forever.

* * * *

All Stars Fall: A Seaside Pictures/Big Sky Novella
By Rachel Van Dyken

From *New York Times* and *USA Today* bestselling author Rachel Van Dyken…

She *left*.
Two words I can't really get out of my head.
She left *us*.
Three more words that make it that much worse.
Three being another word I can't seem to wrap my mind around.
Three kids under the age of six, and she left because she missed it. Because her dream had never been to have a family, no her dream had been to marry a rockstar and live the high life.
Moving my recording studio to Seaside Oregon seems like the best idea in the world right now especially since Seaside Oregon has turned into the place for celebrities to stay and raise families in between touring and producing. It would be lucrative to make the move, but I'm doing it for my kids because they need normal, they deserve normal. And me? Well, I just need a break and help, that too. I need a sitter and fast. Someone who won't flip me off when I ask them to sign an Iron Clad NDA, someone who won't sell our pictures to the press, and most of all? Someone who looks absolutely nothing like my ex-wife.

He's tall.
That was my first instinct when I saw the notorious Trevor Wood, drummer for the rock band Adrenaline, in the local coffee shop. He

ordered a tall black coffee which made me smirk, and five minutes later I somehow agreed to interview for a nanny position. I couldn't help it; the smaller one had gum stuck in her hair while the eldest was standing on his feet and asking where babies came from. He looked so pathetic, so damn sexy and pathetic that rather than be star-struck, I took pity. I knew though; I knew the minute I signed that NDA, the minute our fingers brushed and my body became insanely aware of how close he was—I was in dangerous territory, I just didn't know how dangerous until it was too late. Until I fell for the star and realized that no matter how high they are in the sky—they're still human and fall just as hard.

* * * *

Hold On: A Play On/Big Sky Novella
By Samantha Young

From *New York Times* and *USA Today* bestselling author Samantha Young…

Autumn O'Dea has always tried to see the best in people while her big brother, Killian, has always tried to protect her from the worst. While their lonely upbringing made Killian a cynic, it isn't in Autumn's nature to be anything but warm and open. However, after a series of relationship disasters and the unsettling realization that she's drifting aimlessly through life, Autumn wonders if she's left herself too vulnerable to the world. Deciding some distance from the security blanket of her brother and an unmotivated life in Glasgow is exactly what she needs to find herself, Autumn takes up her friend's offer to stay at a ski resort in the snowy hills of Montana. Some guy-free alone time on Whitetail Mountain sounds just the thing to get to know herself better.

However, she wasn't counting on colliding into sexy Grayson King on the slopes. Autumn has never met anyone like Gray. Confident, smart, with a wicked sense of humor, he makes the men she dated seem like boys. Her attraction to him immediately puts her on the defense because being open-hearted in the past has only gotten it broken. Yet it becomes increasingly difficult to resist a man who is not only determined to seduce her, but adamant about helping her find her purpose in life and embrace the person she is. Autumn knows she shouldn't fall for Gray. It can only end badly. After all their lives are divided by an ocean and their inevitable separation is just another heart break away…

Discover 1001 Dark Nights Collection Six

DRAGON CLAIMED by Donna Grant
A Dark Kings Novella

ASHES TO INK by Carrie Ann Ryan
A Montgomery Ink: Colorado Springs Novella

ENSNARED by Elisabeth Naughton
An Eternal Guardians Novella

EVERMORE by Corinne Michaels
A Salvation Series Novella

VENGEANCE by Rebecca Zanetti
A Dark Protectors/Rebels Novella

ELI'S TRIUMPH by Joanna Wylde
A Reapers MC Novella

CIPHER by Larissa Ione
A Demonica Underworld Novella

RESCUING MACIE by Susan Stoker
A Delta Force Heroes Novella

ENCHANTED by Lexi Blake
A Masters and Mercenaries Novella

TAKE THE BRIDE by Carly Phillips
A Knight Brothers Novella

INDULGE ME by J. Kenner
A Stark Ever After Novella

THE KING by Jennifer L. Armentrout
A Wicked Novella

QUIET MAN by Kristen Ashley
A Dream Man Novella

ABANDON by Rachel Van Dyken
A Seaside Pictures Novella

THE OPEN DOOR by Laurelin Paige
A Found Duet Novella

CLOSER by Kylie Scott
A Stage Dive Novella

SOMETHING JUST LIKE THIS by Jennifer Probst
A Stay Novella

BLOOD NIGHT by Heather Graham
A Krewe of Hunters Novella

TWIST OF FATE by Jill Shalvis
A Heartbreaker Bay Novella

MORE THAN PLEASURE YOU by Shayla Black
A More Than Words Novella

WONDER WITH ME by Kristen Proby
A With Me In Seattle Novella

THE DARKEST ASSASSIN by Gena Showalter
A Lords of the Underworld Novella

Also from 1001 Dark Nights:
DAMIEN by J. Kenner
A Stark Novel

Discover the World of 1001 Dark Nights

Collection One

Collection Two

Collection Three

Collection Four

Collection Five

Bundles

Discovery Authors

Blue Box Specials

Rising Storm

Liliana Hart's MacKenzie Family

Lexi Blake's Crossover Collection

Kristen Proby's Crossover Collection

About Sawyer Bennett

Since the release of her debut contemporary romance novel, Off Sides, in January 2013, Sawyer Bennett has released multiple books, many of which have appeared on the New York Times, USA Today and Wall Street Journal bestseller lists.

A reformed trial lawyer from North Carolina, Sawyer uses real life experience to create relatable, sexy stories that appeal to a wide array of readers. From new adult to erotic contemporary romance, Sawyer writes something for just about everyone.

Sawyer likes her Bloody Marys strong, her martinis dirty, and her heroes a combination of the two. When not bringing fictional romance to life, Sawyer is a chauffeur, stylist, chef, maid, and personal assistant to a very active daughter, as well as full-time servant to her adorably naughty dogs. She believes in the good of others, and that a bad day can be cured with a great work-out, cake, or even better, both.

Sawyer also writes general and women's fiction under the pen name S. Bennett and sweet romance under the name Juliette Poe.

For more information visit https://sawyerbennett.com

For a complete list of books available from Sawyer Bennett, please visit: https://sawyerbennett.com/bookshop/

Code Name: Genesis
A Jameson Force Security Novel
COMING MAY 7, 2019

Joslyn and Kynan's story isn't over. Journey forward nine years to find out what happens to this couple and whether they can be given a second chance at happiness in an exciting new romantic suspense series by Sawyer Bennett.

Code Name: Genesis (A Jameson Force Security Novel), the first full-length novel in the Jameson Force Security Series, releases May 7, 2019.

The alpha men of Jameson Force Security have seen their fair share of nasty stuff, none more than Kynan McGrath. But when he's asked to protect his first love, Joslyn Meyers, from a hell-bent stalker, Kynan is determined to do the job he's hired to do, regardless of their shattered past.

Even though she broke his heart nine years ago, he will stop at nothing to keep her safe. Even if it means giving up his own life in return.

On behalf of 1001 Dark Nights,

Liz Berry and M.J. Rose would like to thank ~

Steve Berry
Doug Scofield
Kim Guidroz
Jillian Stein
InkSlinger PR
Dan Slater
Asha Hossain
Chris Graham
Fedora Chen
Kasi Alexander
Jessica Johns
Dylan Stockton
Richard Blake
and Simon Lipskar

CPSIA information can be obtained
at www.ICGtesting.com
Printed in the USA
LVHW041817140319
610673LV00002B/195